More Books b~ ~~~~ ^ ~~~

Forthcoming

Blueprint Recipes for Life
A DON'T DIE Cookbook

Children's Books

Code 7: Cracking the Code for an Epic Life
(for ages 7-10)

"A suitable addition to any school library that is looking for short but fast-paced stories that reinforce pro-social behavior."
– School Library Journal

The Proto Project: A Sci-Fi Adventure of the Mind
(for ages 9-12)

"Johnson keeps the middle school laughs going in this action-packed, accessible look at the pros and cons of advancing AI and technology, a contemporary tale certain to intrigue and entertain young readers."
– Publishers Weekly

We the People

We the People

By Zero

Venice, CA

WE THE PEOPLE

Library of Congress Control Number: 2023950764

E-book ISBN: 978-1-940556-20-8
Paperback ISBN: 978-1-940556-18-5
Hardcover ISBN: 978-1-940556-19-2

 Published by Zero
protocol.bryanjohnson.com

"The low density of this region is of high statistical significance and does not appear easily reconcilable with any of the popular models for the growth of structure in the universe."

"A Survey of the Boötes Void"
Astrophysical Journal
March 15,1987

§0.00.00

Will we die?

I do not know. Push it.

But....

Push it.

If you are not scared, why am I?

I'm scared. This could be the end of everything. The Pause.

This is our last hope.

Did you p....

§0.01.01

I laughed at the invitation. It was a wasted effort. Nobody except Taiga was within miles of me to see or hear anything I did. Why would I ever leave? First, I scanned through the envelope with an infrared flashlight for electronics. I picked up the envelope with electrostatic-free tongs and held it up to the light through an antique, night-vision monocle that might have been my grandfather's, but who really knew anymore. I was careful not to touch the letter with bare hands. I was sure that if I touched or opened it my exact location would be broadcast. However, if I never got near the envelope with heat or skin, the sensor would never get enough power to turn on. It was the only way to stay truly hidden these days.

Nobody had a hint where I was except my courier. All he knew was that once a month he was to leave all my mail—which these days was mostly fan letters and Adults asking for help—in a waterproof bag at preassigned mooring buoys off the Eastern Seaboard. Even he had no idea where the bag went once it disappeared. He never dreamed, I suspect, that the bag always ended up washing ashore in Svalbard, Norway, a few miles from my cabin where I would wait for it once a month; never imagined that I had trained and domesticated an orca to collect the bag and dive deep into the ocean until the pressure cracked all the electronic trackers inside; never dreamed that I paid the

1

orca in fresh seals that I would leave on the beach, each tied to a stake in the sand.

One day I saw a second, smaller fin waiting in the ocean, this one with what looked like a shotgun blast out of its fin, which worried me. Orcas were known to pass on behaviors to pod members and their calves, so I probably needed to call the whole thing off soon before I lost control. The shotgun blast meant human interaction. The second, smaller orca probably migrated to the Mediterranean during the year and ate the catches off the back of fishing boats until one day a fisherman with Hemingway tattoos and a shotgun had had enough.

I peered through the monocle. From just the first few words of the invitation, I already knew who wrote it and therefore what the rest of it would say. I got enough hints of the world's news from my fan mail that I knew what was happening with the War. The Colonies had won a few months ago. A total surrender by the Adults. The Children had won their way and their rights, but they had no idea what they wanted those to be. They were declaring independence but without a mission, agenda, nation state, or religion.

The whole Convention was probably being organized by Washington, the cleverest of the Colony's twelve leaders but also one of youngest (only eight or nine years old, or around that) so the invitation would probably continue as a churlish recreation of the Bill of Rights, but with basic cognitive freedoms in place of human or personal freedoms.

Washington's humor was predictable humor, but it seemed to work for him. People laughed and it wasn't just because he was in charge. They had laughed with him before he outranked them. Maybe that's why he rose so quickly.

I hadn't laughed much lately but I knew the physical act could be good for me, so instead of wasting metabolic energy on muscle tightening, I induced the positive benefits it would have had with my Bridge alone. I relaxed my muscles, increased my red blood cell count and oxygen intake, and spat out some endorphins until finally— without choosing to, without needing to, without wanting to—I laughed. I surprised myself. Maybe cause and effect were backward on that one; maybe, like fear, the action came after the reaction. Laughter after the laughter response.

I made a mental note to sift through Bridge data on every time I'd laughed since I was born. Later, maybe. After dinner. After I take Taiga for a walk.

To accept the invitation would be foolish and dangerous. I would never accept. I wasn't part of that anymore. I also knew to be wary of sorting through the mail because another of the exact same kind of letter would be in the bag somewhere. I couldn't touch it, either. Washington likely had no idea how to send it to me or when, if ever, I would receive any of the letters. That meant if he really needed me, he sent hundreds throughout the month to various drop locations. I had never responded to any letter, knowing that even a repeated cadence of response or a small change in my dialect or even an analysis of the molecular composition of the ink as it absorbed the Nordic atmosphere could give me away.

At one point, I was the world's best cryptographer and code breaker, but I hadn't spoken to another person or read up on any of the tech in more than two years. I was behind. I had no idea what was state of the art anymore and knew only that I needed to assume that the technologies I don't know about are likely more capable than I could even begin to imagine.

Sure enough, after sorting through some handwritten letters I threw in the box with all the others still unopened, I found another of the exact invitation. The envelope was spare, white, and thick. It had a slightly indented gold imprint on its front with my name in all caps: ADAMS. I ran the tongs across the gold, pretending the tongs were my finger, tracing the envelope's edges. I looked at my watch, just in case. The indents felt good. Tracing my name felt like hearing it and I hadn't heard anyone say my name in more than two years.

I would never go to Washington's victory lap because I knew what they didn't want to admit: They were better off without me. I was a worldwide intellectual and celebrity, yes. More famous than Einstein ever was, but that was mostly because of the constant comparisons to him. My signature would likely convince billions of Adults that the post-War propositions were likely to be fair, reasoned, and have humanity's best interests in mind. I was one of the very few Children whom the Adults sided with occasionally, or at least whose ideas they (used to) tolerate, but that's mostly because I never really fit in with other Children and because I was vocal in my disagreement when they forged off and became Colonists under Washington's leadership. I didn't get along with Children either because, honestly, I didn't understand them. They were just so far behind me intellectually, even though the least-smart Bridged Child was leaps and bounds smarter than even the smartest Adult.

Plus, it was impossible to explain to Children of other ages exactly what it was like to be the only human to have a Bridge for years and years before people had even *heard* of a Bridge, let alone how to optimize childhood learning for one. I'm a bit feral, in that sense, having to grow up with one implanted in me without the social tools to guide its proper use. Raised by wolves. If wolves were a machine-altered subconscious.

I would also never go to Washington's wartime victory lap because I knew my presence in absentia would likely command more authority and weight than if I were to show up in person. It would confuse people to see me again. To see how tall I'd grown, for one—over seven and a half feet—by regulating my growth hormone levels, metabolism, and diet perfectly through puberty. They would want to know what I had been working on, where I had been, how I felt about my sister's death. Blah blah blah. All things that would distract from the task at hand. I would probably have to give a speech. Over-intervention is just as bad as under-intervention. Celebrity members and participants of the Constitution Congress, or whatever Washington was calling it, would be distracted by my celebrity. It would hinder the goal.

Which is why it was such a surprise when a ballistic sphere landed a couple dozen meters outside my cabin. I looked at my watch. Two minutes and forty seconds exactly.

§0.01.02

Taiga growled at the sphere. I walked outside and met it, having pieced most of it together instantly. Ballistic drop ship technology, as I last knew it, could reach anywhere on Earth in under seven minutes. The closest Colony to Svalbard was New Greenland, but they would have launched from New Zemlya or New Japan. The drop ship had landed exactly two minutes and forty seconds after I had touched the gold lettering on the invitation, even though all I did was trace it with the tongs. Which means someone must have some new kind of tracking technology. I should have been more careful. I realized that now.

I shouldn't have stuck to the water-only mail drops. They must have figured out that I was somehow using the ocean and that I would obviously use the bioelectric tongs to test and handle the mail because that is "off-the-grid 101" these days to prevent the tracking pixel embedded in the paper. All they had to do was somehow make the interaction of the tongs the power source to activate the tracker. Maybe by using some static energy or magnetic property? I'd have to look into it. I held the envelope in my hand and considered its chemistry and physics and imagined how it was forged. I couldn't be mad at it. But I threw it in the fire anyway.

I simulated what to do the next time I would try to hide from all of humanity. Next time, I would go with the backup plan, which I knew deep down should have been the original plan. To hide in plain sight, to use people's assumptions that I'm a genius and *trying* to hide and therefore would be super clever and analog about it but instead to do the thing nobody expects, which is to *not* hide. Rather, to hide somehow in plain sight, the brain's largest blind spot. I was the smartest human alive, yes, but I wasn't smarter than two billion Children, all Bridged, who just fought and won the most technologically advanced and brutal war of all time.

The sphere, about the size of a basketball, had landed cleanly. I knew it wouldn't be dangerous. It would have been way easier to bomb me and they wouldn't have missed. They want me alive. They want me to attend the Convention. By now, hundreds of Children would be huddled in command centers in every Colony on Earth, gathered around screens, watching the live feed of the camera on the outside of the drop ship or maybe the satellite feeds.

They probably even had a team of AI and Children scientists of various kinds dedicated to finding me. The effort probably began during the War, when they determined that I was needed for some Manhattan Project-level initiative; probably had some brilliant geneticists to run DNA sentinel scans in every city and town on the planet, in case bits of my DNA floated into the jet stream or ended up in the air; probably had an AI that tracked all of the internet's text for traces of my syntax or prose. There were language robot scramblers these days to "anonymize" one's text and speech patterns, but I'd seen what was possible. I knew to say nothing. I was off the internet entirely.

I waved to the sphere. No use pretending anymore.

"Sit, girl," I said to Taiga.

She calmed instantly once she could see I wasn't worried and instantly, the sphere became a toy to her. It was a perfect sphere, probably a payload of a rocket that separated and dropped from high up in the atmosphere. Taiga sniffed it but still hadn't touched it. She was most curious when she was afraid. (Aren't we all?) From no obvious source, the sphere made a noise. Taiga's ears perked. She growled again and readied her forepaws to sprint or strike.

"Adams, my old boy." It was Washington.

"Washington. Congrats on the victory."

Those damn tongs.

"We've had a lot of people looking for you for a long time," said Washington. "We really could have used your help."

"Is a personnel pod on the way?" I asked.

"It is."

"How much time do I have?"

"About thirty minutes."

"I'm not leaving Taiga."

"You know," said Washington, "if you had helped us with cracking the Adults' quantum codes, we could have ended the war at least a year earlier. That's millions of lives lost. Billions. Children and Adults. Mostly Adults. On *your* conscience."

Washington was never one for small talk. It was beneath him. Beneath all of us, he had said once.

"I don't need moral approbation. I don't need convincing," I responded. "Yes, I will attend the Convention. You don't need to threaten me with exposure or capture or negotiate on emotional terms. We don't need to go down the branches of the game theoretic models your teams and AI experts are feeding you right now. You can see from the satellite data I have nothing. I owe nothing. I need nothing. I love no one. My family is all dead. My friends think I'm a traitor. I have no religion to die for. I barely believe in anything above myself."

"Well, that's a shame," said Washington. He choked lightly on the attack when he said *shame. Sh-uh-ame.* It was only a few tenths of milliseconds of a pause, but it wasn't normal for his speech. I could tell instantly from the small tonal shift that he was going to say something gleeful, something that he had been waiting to say for years, that was so surprising that it overcame his training and his Bridge's best efforts at emotional suppression and operational security.

He was still young. This was a weakness of his. I could use that.

I reduced my adrenal feedback to cortisol in preparation that he might say something so surprising that it caught even me off guard, even as I mentally went through millions of possible things he might say, especially the improbable ones.

Washington went on: "Because your sister's here and she wants to talk to you."

§0.01.03

I tried to not let the shock cloud my thinking. During my brain's development, my Bridge had shunted some neurons to connect otherwise-unconnected regions of the brain, which gave me access to control over the hypothalamic hormonal responses with the same dexterity evolution gave to the human hand. I could control hormone and neurotransmitter release like individual fingers, grasping and releasing as if gliding through treetops.

The reduced adrenal response meant that Washington's statement didn't cause the body-wide cascade that would normally shut down reproduction, ramp up energy usage, and tint certain decision making. Instead, I kicked up some adrenaline and a synthetic form of hyperdopamine I trained my brain to make and use. Much better than the natural stuff. These next few seconds were crucial.

This wasn't a fight-or-flight moment, so I didn't need the mobilization of the stress response. I needed to focus. I needed to think.

"You're lying," I said.

"Don't stall, Adams. That's beneath you. Beneath all of us listening the world over. You have thousands of Children—excuse me, Colonists—listening in right now. You are the biggest news event since the War ended."

Taiga was upset. She could tell something was wrong again, as if she and I had a Bridge connecting us.

Washington continued talking over my silence. "You've already figured out that I wouldn't lie about your sister. That if I ever did that I could do so only once, and your wrath would extend infinitely. You've probably already figured out that your sister, even though she's your twin, is much smarter than you and that she did the thing you didn't seem brave enough to do. She hid in plain sight. No plainer way than to be dead, is there, than to be known the world over as an idea, as a martyr, in everyone's minds? The tragic victim of the assassination that started the worst war in history. The idea that she would fake her death and cause billions of Adults to die in the War was untenable to most. It didn't match her personality. It didn't match her conscience. She would never do that, right? Which is exactly how she got away with it. Using people's assumptions and priors about her personality against her. Hiding in plain sight. And the only person smart enough to piece her plan together—you—was too wracked with guilt, thinking you caused her death, to investigate it dispassionately and rationally. A sort of cognitive purloined letter. Hiding in all our blind spots."

"I know the story," I responded meekly.

"Our team spent so long trying to find you in plain sight, too. We thought you'd do the twin thing, and we knew you two kids loved that story growing up. Her plan was brilliant in retrospect. She threw the entire world off her scent."

"I need to pack some things," I said.

"Great. We have a secure room for you when you get here," said Washington. I knew that he meant it. He knew I was only useful if my thinking was mine alone. He had expected maybe the tiniest bit of resistance, but I knew I was caught. Struggling was a waste.

"I'm not leaving Taiga," I said.

"There's a smaller set of straps for...him? Her?"

"Her."

"I...." Washington paused. He wanted to tell me something that he didn't want to share with everyone else listening.

"You'll tell me in person?" I asked.

"Exactly."

"Where am I going?"

"New Japan. Via New Zemlya."

"I need a favor. No questions asked," I said.

"I will grant it without hesitation."

"No questions asked?"

"None."

"OK. I need my mail forwarded," I said.

"You don't even read it."

"I want to. One day. It's important."

Washington sounded genuinely confused. "We played back the last few years of satellite video from the cabin once we found you. You couldn't possibly have known this, but we seeded all the world's fault lines and volcanoes during the War with emitters that satellites can ping to get more details about what's happening on the surface from

14

both above and below. We can see through cloud cover. We can see through basically everything. Super useful. The point being, we rewound the last two years and watched the videos, and you only collected your mail at night and under heavy cloud cover. We still don't know how it got from the mooring buoys to your little rustic coastal beach, though. What did you do, send yourself a remote submersible every month that drove itself?"

"In a sense. That's actually related to the favor," I said.

I was still stalling for time, of course, plotting any chance at exit, no matter how remote. I couldn't think of anything. The remoteness of my cabin was haunting me. I really was trapped. I continued, "Every month, for one year, starting one month from now, I need you to leave a seal tied to a stake on the beach. After one year, slow the cadence. First to once every other month, then once every three months, and then once a year. The mail will be delivered here usually within twenty-four hours once the seal is tied up. Don't ask how. Then, can you have someone collect it and drop ship it to me wherever I am?"

"Done. I won't even ask," said Washington. "Now stop stalling. Again. And pack. The drop ship will land in a few minutes."

"And after that?"

"We have a few meteoroids circling the globe whose orbits we can decay if we need to make something look like a natural event. You've got two minutes until the drop ship lands. And then you've got, oh, eight minutes or so accord-

15

ing to our ballistics guy here to get everything in the drop ship once it lands. After that, a meteorite about the size of a small car will obliterate your cabin. Leave no trace you were ever there for the Adults to find. If we're lucky, they'll think you're dead too. The rock is already inbound. It even has a name. We can't change its course once we set it so I'd really get to packing if I were you."

"The War changed you, Washington."

"Did it? Maybe it did."

"I don't need anything from inside. I'll just wait here."

"Not your notes? Your research? I was hoping you'd have unified physics or solved some great cryptography problem by now."

"I burn them every night and recreate them in the morning."

"I can't wait to see," said Washington.

I looked up at the clouds. They used to comfort me, but no longer. I remembered seeing a clip of a small boy who testified in international court, in the early days of using drones for war, who spoke of being afraid to go outside when the sky was blue and clear because the drones could see right through the air all the way to him. For two thousand years, from ancient Greece on, blue skies had meant visibility, which meant safety. Now, however, blue skies meant that *the drones could see*, which meant anyone could be stricken from the sky at any time on purpose or by accident, as if by Zeus.

I watched as what looked like a small dark hole opened in the clouds above me. Through it came a glistening silver craft that barely slowed until it slammed into the ground, deformed into what appeared to be a liquid, like a large, metallic drop of water hitting the ground, and then immediately reformed into the shape of a sarcophagus-like pod.

Taiga was still trying to bury the first sphere. "What the hell was that?" I asked.

"Oh, you have much to learn, Adams. It's extremely safe," said Washington, through the sphere beneath Taiga's paws.

She had managed to half bury it.

§0.01.04

A hatch formed along the edges of the new, egg-like drop pod, as if it were being carved out from the inside by welders. Above it, a second drone descended and hovered. That drone had what looked like a large circular magnet, like those used to lift cars in junkyards, on its underside.

Washington went on, trying to calm me. "The liquid graphene can take on any shape. Think of the craft above it like those magnets in car junkyards, except it can pick you up and drop you off anywhere on the planet. You can't see it, but it's attached with a thin liquid wire to webbing we control in the upper atmosphere. Like a private space elevator, if you want to think of it in terms of old tech. A great toy. Oh, and don't be surprised when you slam into the side of the building at high speed in New Zemlya. The building will sort of absorb the ship like a membrane and then spit you out on the inside. The ship becomes the wall. I guess it's more accurate to say the ship started as part of the wall. Anyway, I'll have an engineer show you how it works when you get here. It will make sense when you see it. Just think of it like a cell membrane releasing and absorbing vesicles. I don't understand the chemistry, to be honest, but it has completely changed transportation and cargo shipping. And war ships. And space. No need for a deck to launch anything you want—people, missiles, drones. No need for an airlock in space, which is huge. The only problem is it looks like the skies are full of buckshot now. Just solid spheres running around everywhere, waiting to crash into something with who knows what inside of them."

Taiga seemed to sense that we were going somewhere soon. She went inside the cabin and brought outside her leash, a stuffed coyote chew toy she loved, a pen—my favorite, the one I use every day, which she probably sees as my favorite chew toy—and her bowl of food.

The inside of the pod was minimalist. Nothing but a chair and some straps for me and a harness for Taiga underneath my seat. Washington's voice piped from the inside of the drop pod. It seemed to come from nowhere in particular. Spatial, holographic audio? Last I checked, that was only rumored to be possible. The math was too complicated only two years ago. I made a mental note to research it. Once I got my straps on, I strapped Taiga in and put my hand on her head to calm her. The door sealed around us, as if there had never been an opening.

On the five-minute drop pod journey to New Zemlya, I scanned through my Bridge for the history of every time I'd laughed since I was born. This was one of the benefits of the Bridge. I could run stats on any moment of my subjective life or experience. I ran a correlation to the hormonal and physiological responses known to be produced by laughter and checked if they were time locked to the actual laugh itself. They weren't.

19

So, it was true. I had always had the benefit of laughter before I physically laughed. I took the same analysis and generalized it to all my physical displays of emotion or reaction. It was true for all of them. The response came first, *then* my awareness of it.

I looked down at Taiga. A smile crossed her face as I patted her head. "It's going to be okay, girl. We're almost there," I told her.

§0.01.05

We were not "almost there."

Washington had lied about the final stop being New Japan—he probably lied just in case anyone was listening in. There was absolutely no use in *my* knowing my destination, which meant that there was no reason for him to share it. He often said that information should never be wasted. In this case, it meant that Washington didn't trust all the Children. That's new. It used to be Us versus Them, Big versus Little, Up versus Down.

If Washington presumes some who were watching are spies, it means that some of them probably are. That means *a lot* of people just figured out I'm alive all at once. A spy for the Adults would have broken cover immediately just to get the news out.

"Just a few more minutes, girl," I whispered to Taiga.

I could not see. The pod doubled as a deprivation tank. But there was no mistaking Taiga's behavior. Her head was snapping back and forth in smooth pursuit of *something*, like she was a person sitting at the window of a train watching tree after tree go by at high speed. It was an impossible motion for the mammalian brain to track something like that with the eyes and head unless there was *something* to be tracked. What was she looking at?

I could see nothing, of course. The walls of the pod were sheer and metallic, with absolutely no surfaces, indentations, or scratches. It was like being inside a grey metal soap bubble. Was she watching something on the walls? But there was nothing on the walls.

Taiga's head was slowly tracking left, watching, until it rapidly turned all the way back to the right and started tracking slowly left again.

Her ears were perked. She was hunting.

Which could only mean that Taiga was *watching* the Earth's magnetic lines go by, as if each line was a tree outside the window on a train. There had been rumors that some dogs and cows, like pigeons, lined up along magnetic fields to sleep, which means they must have magneto-receptors in their brains to gather information that is invisible to us. Being born with magnetoreceptors was sort of like being born with a Bridge—the brain will use whatever information it can to make sense of the world. Doesn't matter if it comes from light, sound, UV, touch, Bridge, magnetic fields. It all works, as long as it's useful.

So *that's* how Taiga found her way back to me during a snowstorm last year. She knew exactly how to get home. She just followed the Earth's built-in map.

"You're just like a homing pigeon, aren't you, girl?"

Taiga broke her concentration from the magnetic lines and looked up at me. Presuming that she was seeing a field line, which are evenly threaded around the Earth, I calculated from the cadence of her head movements that we must be going around 800 miles per hour, about twice as fast as a commercial plane and just barely over the sound barrier. An odd speed. Why go slightly *above* the sound barrier, and alert everyone to the pod's presence?

I snapped back into my brain. One of the consequences of being born with a Bridge is that the part of my brain wired to mentally and visually imagine things got a few extra wires hooked up to the visual cortex, which actually perceived things. So, when I close my eyes and imagine, I *see.* It's not just some lame, barely Technicolor, lo-res trace of a visual memory. It's as good as being there. Daydreaming was very convincing, and one of the biggest challenges I have is not getting lost in the rich, imagined world of daydreams.

Taiga growled. Something had changed. My stomach dropped and we fell from the sky. We were in a freefall and the pod started shifting the shape of its walls to be more aerodynamic. We had taken on a projectile shape, hurtling through the sky. My vision blurred. And then, suddenly, all was calm. We had stopped.

Before I could unharness, the metallic wall in front of me sort of just opened. "Dissolved" is perhaps a better word. The wall of the pod *became* the wall we had hit and the ship we used to be in was now contiguous with the wall of the craft. It was all very strange, like the solution to some smartass riddle. Without ever passing through a doorway, I was suddenly inside.

Two male Children, both around age ten, greeted me. They wore all-black tactical suits and each had many medallions on their lapels, which meant nothing to me except that they were military. As expected, they startled at my height. If the timeline was right, I was the only Bridged child (except my sister, of course) to hit puberty. The oldest of the other Children would be, what, eleven years old? There may have been a few more children secretly implanted with a Bridge, but I doubted it. All the early trials went to Adults, but Bridges didn't work on Adults.

"Sir," said one of the military boys, who then went silent. Probably low ranking. Didn't seem comfortable saying anything outside of protocol. This single infantry boy was probably smarter than any human who had ever lived prior to 2030, yet the primate in him still made him defer to rank and hierarchy. How silly it all is. The other boy looked at him, then back at me, and spoke: "Welcome to New Zemlya, sir. This will be your home for the next few weeks."

"Forgive the precaution," said the first to speak, but now with a new stammer. "But we need to check you for weapons and any electronics. If you'd be so kind as to just turn them over, we can save ourselves any hassle."

"I have nothing on me," I said, holding my arms high. "Just this pen. I've been off the grid for two years. Nothing electronic. No weapons except a bow and arrow and spear I left behind."

I held the pen to the soldiers, who ignored it. I glanced around at the landing area. We were inside, clearly. The light was all artificial. The size and hum of the air vents meant we were probably underground with filtered air piped in. In the medium distance, Children of all sizes had stopped to gawk. I knew it. I was going to be a distraction around here.

"We're underground?" I asked.

"Yes, sir. You didn't feel or notice when the pod went underwater?"

"I hadn't, no."

I followed the two military boys without a word. Clearly, I was to do as I was told until more was explained. Taiga walked excitedly alongside us. She hadn't seen anything but Norway, me, and the cabin for two years.

"During the descent," continued the soldier, "the pod broke the ocean's surface and melded with the landing pad here. We are deep under the island of Nova Zemlya. In its crust. The only secure way in or out is by landing on the wall there behind you with one of the drop pods. There's an encryption key built into the structure of the craft itself. The only metal that can fuse with it is metal that came from it. This is the most secure military base on Earth, by far."

"On Earth?" I said, playfully.

The soldier said nothing. This was another problem with celebrity. When they were so eager to impress me, they let secrets spill without even noticing. Anybody would. It's built into our basic default code. They knew everyone would be vying for my attention and succor and they individually wanted to stand out, somehow; to be remembered by me for something. I just had to stand there silently and let the secrets happen. Honeypotting without any of the hard work.

As I looked more carefully around the room where we landed, which was about the volume of a large sports stadium, I noticed that other than the air ducts there was only one way out, a tunnel bored through a rock wall. My comparison to a sports stadium wasn't too far off. A large green field was in the center of the room. Ten Children were doing what looked like drills under the command of a teenager with a whistle who seemed to be coaching them all. The soldiers were clearly escorting me through the tunnel.

"This base is huge," I said.

"What? Oh, this is just the welcome mat," said one.

"Is that some sort of military training?" I asked, gesturing to the field.

"No, that's Zero Ball. Originally called ŭr-Senet, but nobody likes pronouncing the 'ŭr' part, which just meant 'zero' anyway. It's a game specifically designed to be difficult for robot AI, so humans stand a chance. Team game. Five on five on five, usually with one AI team."

"For balance?" I asked.

"Exactly. It's designed from the concept of Rock-Paper-Scissors equilibrium. If there are three populations of bacteria—"

"I know the mechanism," I said. "If two bacterial col-onies are fighting on a hillside, the one with the slightest advantage will always, eventually, win. Creating a monoculture. But if there's three species, and each has an advantage and disadvantage over the other, nobody can outcompete the other two at once and all three can coexist."

"Exactly. Except, well, the AI still kicked everyone's ass until we figured out how to—"

The other soldier forcefully and quickly lifted his hand as a fist, a signal the other immediately took to mean "stop." All three of us stopped and stood perfectly still as the man with his first up pointed to the ceiling. Taiga looked up, worried. But I knew a red herring when I saw one. Grice would be proud. The guard had intended to stop the other from revealing what it was they figured out how to do and was just gesturing up to the ceiling to make me think the "stop" command was about some imminent threat.

Not that yet another secret was about to be spilled. But this was, in their own words, the safest place on the planet. Nobody would be vigilant like that in a place his brain knew was safe. That's not how brains worked. I couldn't tell which boy was which anymore as they walked on either side of me, with Taiga somehow leading the way while being led, which was her specialty.

"Are there other dogs down here?" I asked.

"No. No. Not since...well, maybe President Washington can tell you more. What I know is above my security clearance."

"I appreciate the candor," I said.

§0.01.06

I kept glancing back at the field where Zero Ball was being played. There was something very odd about the drills, which looked highly synchronized. The whole team was standing still with their hands in front of them, moving their fingers rapidly, as if playing piano in the air. The synchronization was remarkable. Every movement of each person, down to their posture and the way they held their heads and bodies, was identical. They weren't just *mostly* in sync. They were *entirely* in sync. Extremely diligent coaching, I imagined.

"They're very coordinated," I said.

"Oh, you have no idea," said one of the soldiers, as we approached the tunnel. It was a huge tunnel, as wide as a five-lane highway and maybe six stories tall. Children in Zero Ball uniforms—about half of them boys, half girls; the girls towering in height above the boys by at least a few inches—were running in formation, exiting the tunnel toward the field. They, too, were extraordinarily synchronized in their movements. It seemed as if when one of the girls at the front of the runner pack turned to look at Taiga, they all did, wide-eyed, in unison.

The inside of the tunnel was coated with the same metallic stuff the drop pod was made from. I ran my hands along it to be sure. Same stuff. And then, like a ghost walking through a wall, an aneurysm in the wall appeared and spat out a smiling, lithe Washington.

"Whoa, look at the size of you!" he shouted.

He never stopped smiling as he greeted me, shook my large, sinewy hand with both of his in one grasp. He didn't need to bend down very far to reach the top of Taiga's head, if at all.

"You may have noticed a few stares," said Washington. "Technically, all non-human animals are banned on the base. We made an exception for you. They haven't seen a non-VR dog in over a year, most likely."

"Why are they banned?"

"Oh, that's classified," said Washington, still beaming. His hand was hanging in the air where it had been to shake mine, as if he hadn't even noticed we stopped shaking. He couldn't stop staring at me.

"I see," I said. I couldn't have expected to just be brought into the fold so quickly.

"It's so good to see you, Adams," said Washington as he turned around toward the opposite end of the tunnel. "Follow me. We walk everywhere around here, to keep the blood flowing."

"The base, it's sort of…"

"Termitic? I know. First thing I thought, too, that we, like the cockroaches and ants and termites before us, figured out tunneling as a last resort for our very survival."

"But the surface is habitable?"

29

"Yes, but too hard to hide up there. You know that well, by now."

I could tell that Washington needed this moment. It was quite the discovery, both finding me and getting me here in one piece. But the fact that he seemed to *need* it, a small victory, meant that things might be shakier than his youthful confidence belied. Why would he need a small victory like me after leading and winning the most difficult, bloody war in human history? If the letters I had read in Norway were to be believed, it meant that more than three billion Adults had died in the War before they surrendered. Why was everybody beaming and smiling around here? Where was the sorrow or the immense sense of human tragedy and loss? The feeling that things would never be the same? It was so easy to demonize the Adults, even though they created the Bridge technology.

My height might work against me here. I was at least two feet taller than anyone around me, which meant I looked more like an Adult than a Child. It could even be argued that having controlled my hormones like on a studio amplifier for the past two years, making sure that I was cognitively and physically in tune, I was, in fact, more Adult than not. Was that going to be a problem?

It certainly would be in a few years.

"One thing," said Washington. "We need Taiga to see the vet today before she can stay with you. Just a precaution. Make sure she doesn't have any diseases or tracking chips. You know the drill."

"Not without me present," I said.

"Fine, fine. That's fine."

"We could even...no, no. I'll wait."

"Oh, just tell me. You clearly want to."

Washington stopped. His expression got serious, and he looked at each of the guards, who backed away instantly and turned around. Like the start to any offensive joke, Washington looked behind him to see if anyone else was listening or nearby. They weren't. He whispered in my ear: "Look, pets aren't banned because we don't like pets. They're not allowed because we figured out how to Bridge them to their owners and it turned out to be rather unwise. *Very* unwise."

I was surprised. Bridge-Bridge communication, or Crossing, between two brains was thought to be a psychosis-inducing nightmare. Nobody had ever tried it after the early days because it led to madness one hundred percent of the time—a brain could not or would not embed with another. Nobody knew exactly why but there were theories. One was that every brain develops its own kind of code to communicate with itself, which is garbled with connection to any other signal from any other Bridge. As if the encryption key to thought was unique—one per brain.

"I know. I know what you're thinking," said Washington. "That a Crossing makes you mad, right? Well, not *always*. Did you notice those kids playing ŭr-Senet? Zero Ball?"

"I did," I said. I didn't see the connection, though.

31

"Did you notice anything odd about them?"

"They seemed to move perfectly in sync at times, as if one person had control of all their marionette strings."

"Good, good. I thought you'd spot it right away. Zero Ball is such a complicated, difficult sensorimotor and strategic game that AIs were kicking our asses for years. We didn't stand a chance. Our best team didn't even qualify for the top tournaments worldwide. It was all AI teams. But someone had an idea. What if we took the tech to Bridge to pets—which at that stage was barely outside the laboratory— and *connected* the Bridges of all five teammates?"

"They would go insane," I said. "That's an impossible motor control problem. Not even a Bridged human brain can handle that. It would descend into madness instantly."

"Well, you are partially right," said Washington. "No *single* human brain can handle it. But five, working together, to heal and learn and repair? If the computation was distributed? Maybe, right? So, anyway, all the teams have them now and the training is not actually to synchronize their movements. That's easy. It's to learn how to *desynchronize* their movements. When they are rookies, when they first Cross, which is what we call it, they all move exactly in step like they all have one brainstem controlling everything. If you sat the five of them in front of five different pianos, they would all play the same piece of music. Which of course is totally useless for sport. So, most of the training involves getting them to work together in a coordinated, but not *too* coordinated, way."

32

My mind spun with the implications. Of course, they had tried with more than five. Did it work with adults, or did the Crossed Children have to grow up together?

"I don't mean to jump ahead a bit," I said, "but if I hear you right, and presume that you wouldn't ever just use this tech for sport, presumably you already have trials where you've given newborns and infants these, what do you call them, Crossings?"

Washington was silent. Which said all I needed to know.

"Which means," I continued, "that it probably doesn't work so well if you Cross already-formed Children, right?"

More silence. Washington was as stern as I've ever seen him.

"And so," I continued. "You see the writing on the wall, right? What led the Children to break away from the Adults? Because the Bridge didn't work well in Adults. Once they were past the critical period, their brains couldn't handle all the new information. The Adult brain was too set in its ways. But now you're just repeating the cycle, aren't you? The new ones, with the Crossings, are going to just rebel against us Children, who will by that time be the simple bad guys with silly, first-generation Bridges."

"We have a scenario planned for this, Adams," said Washington, with clearly feigned bravado. "Admittedly, it took us a while to realize what you just realized in seconds. You're right, the early Crossings didn't fit in."

"Where are they now?"

"Let us change the subject," said Washington. "Where is Taiga?" I looked around me. Taiga was gone.

"Oh, she's fine," I said. "She disappears all the time. Her herding genes. She needs to know how big this place is first before she can calculate where to put everyone."

Washington laughed.

"You know, the Bridge-to-Bridge only worked, at first, in dogs with their masters. Not chimps. Not horses. Pigs. Cats. We tried everything. There's something special in a dog's evolved sense of social cues. As if their brains share a language. We think the Bridge requires the same underlying mechanism, whatever that is."

"Well, they're the only non-human to understand pointing," I said, waving in the direction of the red herring soldier, who still had his back turned. "Like my escort here. The one who points at ceilings to try to distract me."

"Oh, Adams. I missed your brain," said Washington in a brotherly tone. Suddenly, he got more somber. "Yeah, so, Adams, I may have misled you over the phone. The Convention is real. The need is real. The War is over, and we need to settle the new world order. At the end of the week we *will* be declaring basic universal rights to free and independent thought, free from the constraints of our primitive, hegemonic brains. But we have a bigger problem, Adams. The Convention is just an excuse to gather the best minds in the world without drawing too much attention."

"So much duplicity at so many scales," I said. "Aren't you confident enough with your victory to just be honest with everyone at this point? Isn't that one of the few benefits of winning?"

Washington took the jab in stride. He was maturing.

"I know this is all new for you, Adams. I know your playful, loner side will find times and ways to come out. But something very serious happened at the end of the War. There is, in fact, a reason we are all still underground. All the leadership and cabinets across the Twelve Colonies all got Crossed during the War as soon as we figured out how to do so. We all Crossed in specialized, need-to-know groups. Just like we were teams in Zero Ball, which is how it all started. And, of course, it's irreversible once you do it. It updates the Bridge firmware. No going back. No reversion without taking the whole thing out, which, as you know, is impossible."

Washington paused here, waiting for my response to this last comment. I made no sounds or gestures. He knew my parents had spent years researching how to uninstall a Bridge when they had first invented it. But nobody alive, outside my sister and me, knew what came of those efforts.

We exited the other end of the metallic tunnel into the largest indoor room I had ever seen. An entire city could fit inside. In fact, one did. The tunnel exit was at a slight elevation, with stairs leading down to the expansive, modern city.

"So," continued Washington, "the problem is that the Adults did something rather clever and beautiful. We hadn't thought of it at the time, but Zero Ball would end up our downfall. Do you see why already, Adams?"

"No," I said. I really didn't.

"The game," said Washington, "gave the AIs a perfect reward signal for hacking Bridges. It's the ideal scenario for the AIs. All they needed was an easy way to tell success from failure. They ran trillions of simulations on how to win and the easiest way to win was to hack the communication of the Crossings, like tapping into an undersea cable and listening in. Nobody had thought of Zero Ball as our weakest link. We thought it was outside the game, but it wasn't. It's like how researchers were surprised when the first neural network that learned to play Atari figured out that it could play forever and never lose by simply pressing pause. The goals were misaligned. When our Crossed played in the World Cup competition, it was like a signals intelligence field day for the AI, and thus the Adults. In fact, I think they kept fielding losing teams every year just to keep the illusion up that they cared to win. They weren't even trying to win. They were just scouring every possible frequency range for our encrypted communications, which the AIs then hacked in the name of winning the game."

"And, because you used the same underlying Bridge technology for your own military and social communications—"

"Exactly."

"Which means?"

"We think...well, we think the Adults can read our thoughts," said Washington. "The War might be over, technically. But we are about to enter a long, dark Cold War."

"Do the other Children know?"

"No, only a select handful."

"Will you tell people at the Convention? This could have implications for what it means to have free, independent cognition, yes?"

"Nobody will know unless they need to," said Washington. "I trust you to keep it to yourself. It would not be pretty. What could be more terrifying than having your thoughts read? What if there is another war? How do you defeat an enemy who can read your thoughts?"

I said, "I see. This is troubling indeed. When do we start?"

"The Convention starts tonight."

"Where is everybody then?"

"They're arriving now. Soon. Many have already arrived. We have a quorum."

"Arrived via metallic pod?"

"Oh no, there's a normal airport and door up top, on the surface. Most Children will come in through that. You came in through the—how should I say it?—servant's entrance. The invisible entrance, as it were, for VIPs. The one we use when we don't want to spoil surprise arrivals."

"I see."

I saw Taiga off in the distance and called to her.

She had collected a crowd of Children who thought they were petting her but were really, as a group, being herded into a group. One stood out, a child with a lab coat, who seemed more interested in holding Taiga still than petting her. I called again, and she came running. There were so many hidden human needs. The need to pet a dog, the need to share secrets with a mysterious seven-foot-tall celebrity.

"Should we go to the vet before I see my quarters?" I asked.

Washington went quiet for a second, as if listening to an earpiece. The kind of quiet that means a brain is listening intently with little other bandwidth available to it. At the same time, the Child with a lab coat was touching *his* ear and standing quite still, as if also listening.

"No, no," said Washington, after a moment. "We trust you two. Not a big deal. No vet required. We need to get on with the show."

Something was niggling at my brain. A red-hot error signal that someone was pulling something over on me or that I wasn't being told the whole truth. I called up in my mind's eye a replay of everything that had happened since I landed. I called up a Bridge program I wrote as a young teenager that searched my recent memory for semantic and logical incompatibilities, but the program found none.

Still, something didn't make sense. As fancy as Bridges are, nothing beats mammalian intuition for that strange sensation of something being wrong even if you can't quite place it.

Wait a second.

If there were no pets, why did they have a vet's office?

I looked down at Taiga. She was smiling, staring directly at me. Her eyes had changed to an unmistakable color, an inevitable consequence of the viral protein used in the procedure that injected its cargo into all central nervous systems cells, including the eye.

Taiga was Bridged.

§0.01.07

I tried to ignore what I had just figured out, but Washington wouldn't let me.

"It's standard," he said. "I'm sorry I wasn't more forthcoming, but I knew you would resist. Taiga's Bridge will take a couple days to settle in, but I think you'll be quite pleased after that."

I had already tamped down any anger response, knowing it would do no good. The procedure was irreversible. Wasted emotion was a sunk cost. Besides, I had let Taiga wander off through lack of vigilance. I was to blame.

"You are probably just at the point where you come to terms with the fact that we were going to find a way to do it eventually," said Washington. "Which is true. There's no way you could have been by her side all the time. The question you should be spending more time on is—"

He was right. "*Why* you needed to," I interrupted.

"Exactly."

"And, why?"

A crowd of Children had gathered to gawk at me as Washington and I walked slowly forward, Taiga nipping alternately at the two military guards' heels. They were in a protective formation around Washington—around me too, which was interesting—but as a group we were not in a single file. Taiga preferred single file.

"Any guess?" said Washington. "It's sort of fun, being so close to you again. I forget what it's like to have a human mind that can run circles around even mine."

"I'm out of practice," I said.

"Oh, I doubt that."

There were a few possibilities. One, the simplest, is that Bridge tech for dogs is sort of like a tracking or security device. Maybe once the Bridge kicked in, I could see through her eyes, in a manner of speaking. Play fetch with memories. Open a whole new way of bonding and interacting with her.

Still, a few nefarious possibilities came to mind. Maybe accessing Taiga's memories would give them clues to how I spent the last few years; or maybe they would use the ability to make Taiga suffer as a coercion for me to cooperate. But the hospitality so far seemed to argue against that. Why be so nice when it would be so easy to use force? The human brain was very good at only a few things, one of them being counterfactual simulations. I ran through a few other simulations of how this all might go if they hadn't Bridged her and compared the two possible futures.

"Well," I said, "I think, very shortly, after you give me a rundown of the status of the Colonies and a brief primer on who is attending the convention and what your goals are, you are going to offer me a Crossing with Taiga. I would guess that no matter what you show me in terms of schematics or data or the math for how Bridges and Crossings work, that there is a subjective aspect to it that must be experienced rather than known in the purely academic sense. Probably, more so than any other human except myself and my sister, Taiga's and my brains are already melded a bit, or at least we communicate with some sort of unique, shared code, which your data says makes a Crossing easier or more durable or something. Plus, I imagine there would be a security risk if I Crossed with any of the other Children here, given that I would probably figure out a way to hack their memories of this place quickly. Maybe you don't want that to happen. Or maybe that would make me vulnerable to being hacked and you don't actually trust everyone here."

Washington silently kicked a stone under his foot. I was right, at least about that last bit. Washington's hands were behind his slim frame, one wrist tightly in the other palm, in a pose of measured restraint. He didn't seem to do what the shorter Adults did, which was puff themselves or look up. Washington kept his shoulders curved inward to his chest as if he lived his life having to hunch. He somehow seemed smaller than the other Children of the same size. Taiga nipped at his foot and ran after the small rock he had kicked.

I continued, "So, the safest, simplest, quickest way to get me to understand what it is like to be Crossed is to Cross me with Taiga, knowing it's the only Bridge-to-Bridge I would say yes to at least exploring. That it was also the safest and most likely to work is just a bonus. Plus, you're probably right, I bet I'm going to love it and be grateful. It might even make me trust you and this more easily."

Washington took a deep breath and exhaled. Like he had just been physically overwhelmed and came up for air.

"What I like so much about listening to you," he said, "is that, like a great chess master, you just seem to alight, effortlessly, on the one or two best, or most likely, or truest, of all the theories of mind and possibilities for why things might happen. Especially so when it involves *people*. How do you do it? AIs are great when things are finite, and the rules are clear and when the reward is obvious. Bridged Children are great at understanding physics, science, math, sport, etc. But so few people, even the best and brightest of the Children, when we Cross them together and have their minds literally working together, get *people* right. But you do. It's like you can mentally model other minds so well that their thoughts are just as predictable as guessing where a thrown ball might land. My entire mind of thought and intention is just a simple physics problem to you, isn't it?"

The truth of it was, I didn't know how I knew people so well. I just did. Intentions, motivations, trickery, and meaning just always seemed obvious to me.

Maybe it was directly related to intelligence, but I doubted it. That I was *also* the smartest person in the world was probably just a coincidence. Or maybe it was like that adage about height, that tall people understand more because they've literally been all lesser heights. Maybe I, too, have been all the other IQs. But I knew that wasn't how consciousness or intelligence worked. It wasn't linear.

"I didn't exactly hear a confirmation anywhere in there, did I?" I asked, playfully.

"No, of course not. I'm in the 'neither confirm nor deny' phase of your tour," said Washington.

I had to remind myself that we were all still Children at the end of the day. Immaturity was sure to bleed through, no matter how seriously we took ourselves or our tasks.

"People are gathering," I said, gesturing with my hand off to the distance.

"Yes. You are quite the celebrity," said Washington.

Washington seemed lost in thought. Almost suddenly sad.

"All twelve colonies are here today?" I asked.

"They're already here, yes. Waiting for us, in fact. For you. For the *great seven-foot-tall Adams.*"

Ah, so *that's* what he was melancholic about. His grasp on leadership was slipping and the fervor of the other Children when they saw me was obvious even to him as a kind of social status he couldn't capture anymore. Wrapped in this fervor was awe; wrapped in the awe was permission; wrapped in the permission was submission. I know what he had lost or perhaps never had. The ineffable quality of natural, unforced, status. I, without a military backing, without a position or rank and with reputation alone, could probably take command of all the Colonies in the right circumstances.

Sensing this, Washington would likely try to chop me down a few ranks in the eyes of the Convention attendees. Or he might attempt some sort of basic, primate dominance display—his chimpanzee politics was likely only academic at this point. He was still a Child, with Child hormones, despite his fierce intellect.

He would, I gathered, as a student of history and under the guise of magnanimity and kinship, propose to elect me as chair or president of the Convention as a sort of titular, honorary figurehead. Which left me with only two options. To decline, which would make me look reticent and weak, as if I was past my prime; or to accept and make a fool of myself by getting thrown into the crucible of a world I don't understand and haven't paid attention to in two years.

Instead, he surprised me: "We've already reached quorum, as of a few hours ago, and decided on a few organizational matters. I'm chair of the Convention. Each of the twelve colonies is represented by between one and four of its citizens. Wait, Adams, what do you even know about the Twelve Colonies anymore?"

"There were a few hints and pieces in the letters I received in Norway," I said. "I presume they are all still in the same spots? We didn't lose any actual ground in the War, did we?"

I watched Washington watch my face as I said "we" for the first time in years. I remembered how his invitation had opened:

We the Children, in order to form a more perfect union....

Was I still one of the Children? I was less worried about whether I had changed much in the past two years—really, all I did was make fires, read, and work on the hardest math and philosophy problems—than how much *they* had changed. They had fought while I hid. My escape and hiding out was the biggest mark against me in terms of any lingering fealty to me and likely made my celebrity rather fickle. In certain pockets of Children, I was surely thought of as a coward who never helped when it mattered most. If I was once revered like Einstein, I certainly had shown my colors under pressure. Einstein wrote a letter to the U.S. government about the possibility of the atom bomb just before World War II. And here I was, abstaining from the next big one.

"It's still all the same islands, yes," said Washington. "That was key strategically. As soon as we had space, cyber, and naval dominance, there was almost nothing the Adults could do to get to us. We owe it all to Admiral Maher, in a way, who years ago suggested the Colonies stick to islands for strategic and economic reasons. At the time, consensus was that we invade the mainland. We thought he just liked being alone and staring out at horizons. But he saw what nobody else did, inheriting how the United States Navy treated Japan after World War II, as an unsinkable aircraft carrier. So, we brought the War to them. The major battles were always on *their* lands, not ours. In *their* networks, not ours. They had undersea cables and we had every satellite, vintage and new, and owned everything from the entire stratosphere to the Moon."

"I received a lot of letters asking for help. Mostly from Adults," I said.

"I know."

"You do?"

"We didn't know where you were but we did know your mail drop locations," said Washington. "We read a few of them just to learn what you might learn. Replicated a few. You know, drop a few fake ones in there, to keep you guessing."

"You know, I hadn't thought you'd be spoofing fan mail to mislead me. I'm impressed."

"Not mad?"

"No, not at all. That's rather clever. What was the plan? To lure me out of the foxhole? What sort of stuff did you fake?"

"Well, for one, that the War was over."

I stopped. Paled.

§0.01.08

"Not over?" I asked.

Washington didn't miss a step: "I'm afraid so, Adams. We need you. Now. More than ever."

"What's all this about a Cognitive Constitution, then?"

"Oh, that's happening *also*. We intend to win the War. We need the cognitive charter ready when we do. It's a good cover to get all the smartest minds from each of the colonies here at the same time."

"Then why am I here?"

"You're so smart and you haven't figured it out?"

"I...no—"

"It's your sister."

"What about her? She's here, right?"

Washington looked up, stared me straight in the eyes. He looked so small, like a rock.

"Oh, my sweet boy," he said. "She *used* to be. Used to be in charge of special projects, too. Like Skunkworks, DARPA. But, during the war, she defected and has been, we presume, working with the Adults ever since. That's when everything changed. We thought we had won the War easily, but we think she's the one who helped the AIs figure out how to hack the Crossings and the Bridges. We don't know the extent of the damage but she's probably listening in on all our thoughts, right now, as we speak. *As we think.* I, too, am Crossed, of course. It seemed such a great idea at

48

first, to network my brain into my military comm; achieve sub-millisecond thresholds and decision making."

"But we're underground," I protested. The surprise was too much, too fast, for even my Bridge. This was the one-in-a-trillion outcome. No simulation saw it coming. "No electromagnetic signals can escape. There's no way to send information in or out, right? That's the whole point, isn't it?"

"We thought so, too. But she knows. She knows. They know. The Adults seem to know our every move. We have ways of hiding some plans, but it's onerous. She might be looking at you through my eyes right now. Through *my* Bridge. You might want to say 'Hi,' just in case."

All at once the essence of Washington in my mind's eye changed. He wasn't just Washington, but also with some non-zero probability, also Maddy. It was like a doubly exposed photograph or that rabbit-duck illusion or the Necker Cube. I flipped back and forth between perceiving Washington as Washington but also as both, as if Maddy was superimposed. *Inside* Washington, somehow.

"Why proceed with all this, then?" I asked, still in shock. "Why give away strategy and the Convention if you're all hacked?"

"What else can we do?" asked Washington. He seemed remarkably at peace with the whole thing. "It's a feeling humanity has gotten used to for millennia. Might even be built into us at this point to come to terms with the idea that someone is listening and watching our every move.

Think of the Ancient Greeks. Or any major religion. They assumed that God, or gods, were listening in on their every move and thought but they still went about their days, didn't they? It's been a few weeks now since we realized it and, I must say, it's almost comforting in a way. I never feel alone. You don't know this yet, but one of the best parts of a Crossing is the immense dissipation of loneliness. People always thought it would be terrifying to share thoughts with another mind, but it's actually a remarkably freeing experience."

My theory of mind skills broke at the new reality of its task. Washington's mind perhaps being peered into by the Adults also meant that Washington, if he had a plan at all, was intentionally not saying everything he wanted to say. He knew he was being listened in on, so his *real* plan had to go unstated.

There was no way to communicate it through sign language or subtle body cues because those would be just as accessible to the hackers as normal language. *It meant that he couldn't ever even think of his actual plan.* He knew I knew of his passion for Grice and the information theory of language, which was a start. It meant he knew I knew all this and would know he did too. I would have to sit down and list out the things I knew for certain and things I didn't, in terms of what was and was not some sort of signal. How would he signal me a plan that he wasn't even allowed to think about?

50

Logically, it seemed impossible. It would have to be in the grand gestures. The very act of bringing me here was a kind of communication. The mention of the fact that my Bridge was old—practically analog by the most recent tech standards—was maybe a clue. Maybe my Bridge wouldn't be susceptible to the hack given its age? Bridging Taiga was also surely part of it. That couldn't be for nothing. The big picture was clear, though. I was here for a very specific reason and that reason had nothing to do with the Convention.

Nobody would tell me why. I was going to have to figure it out on my own.

"Well, that's terrifying," I said.

"What can you do?" said Washington, with a resigned shrug.

"And you *know* she's working for the Adults? That's so unlike Madeleine."

Washington winced and slowed again, as if in pain.

"We highly suspect she is. Okay, here goes. Yes, we do know. I've been hiding this from my own thoughts so she wouldn't know, but here we go. Ready?"

"What? What do you mean?"

Washington looked strained. He shook his hands and fingers, like they were on fire, or were returning from being numb.

"Well, one of the reasons we think we've been hacked is because if any Child thinks about Madeleine, their mind is instantly flooded with terrible, depressing thoughts. Painful ones. The worst a brain can come up with and, believe me, brains are *good* at it. It's like a form of conditioned or operant punishment. Like an electric collar, but for the mind, and it seems to be tied to thoughts of her. If anyone fantasizes about her. Thinks about hurting her. Thinks about capturing her. Literally anything about her. Their thoughts afterward turn dark and haunted. It takes a lot of willpower to shove them aside and most can't do it. I can't. I'm suffering immensely right now just telling you about this, as soon as I began thinking about her and we began talking about her."

"And when you mentioned her on the satellite call to me, with everyone listening in?"

"Oh, that was necessary. It caused an ocean's worth of panic over here, but it was worth it. I knew I needed to say it for you to get into the drop ship calmly. We have a few crude workarounds. The smartest ones here have their Bridges acoustically filter her name. Literally, they can't hear the phonemes. The word 'Madeleine' is simply removed from what the brain hears."

"Software? Hardware?" I asked.

"It's new hardware. We don't trust software anymore. We can't."

"And why don't you have that personally installed so you don't feel the pain?"

"I don't believe in it. I believe in suffering. I believe I should suffer because I opened us up to this. I trusted

Madeleine. I...I don't...I don't want the world filtered to me. I want to experience the discomfort fully."

"But the world is massively filtered already, Washington. That's the point of the brain, to filter out the unnecessary parts of the overly complicated world. This is all an illusion, you know."

"Of course. Of course." Clearly, he was in deep psychic pain. He had paled in the last few minutes since the mention of Madeleine and slowed his walk. "But the whole point of the pain, as I interpret it, is to make it so that we forget she's in our heads listening. That's the goal. For her to disappear again but even more deeply. She disappeared once physically, but we all remembered her. Honored her, even. But to *truly* disappear she needs to disappear from thoughts. But I am the leader of the Children. I am the leader of the Colonies. I need to not forget. She's out there and she's dangerous."

"So what's happening right now, in your head? Tell me what you see."

"You don't want to know, Adams. Trust me. You don't want to know. We have people working on finding her and whatever hack she installed or how she did it, but it's not fun work, as you can imagine. The closer they get, the worse their mental punishment seems to be. It's medieval. It's Dante. It's the tenth circle."

"Why not just have non-Crossed people work on it? Non-Bridged?"

"All Children are Bridged."

"But not all Bridges are compromised, right? Only the Crossed ones between people?"

Washington sighed.

"We—"

"You are all Crossed," I interrupted.

"Most, yes. Not all, but most. Ninety-nine-point-nine percent."

"Fascinating. It's a kind of hiding, isn't it? The ultimate purloined letter. Or its opposite? I can't tell. She created a mental blind spot, mental dark matter, and is hiding there. Hiding exactly where everyone knows you are but where nobody dares go."

"Well, sure. It's fascinating until you think about what could be done with it. What if it was more than just her? What if entire groups of people could be eliminated the same way? Entire races? Entire genders? Extinguished from the mind's eye like a candle."

"Cognitive extinction."

"Exactly."

"So, is the pain growing right now? The longer this conversation goes on?" I asked.

"I only have a few minutes or so left before it becomes existentially unbearable. Even now, my Bridge is working overdrive to keep it just so I can say a few coherent words. In an hour or so, I'm going to be so exhausted from the effort that I'll need to hypersleep."

Washington had sat down, as if woozy. His hands and arms were trembling, and his torso, thin as a beanpole, started rocking back and forth. His guards seemed to understand intuitively. He was thinking about Maddy. I placed a hand on his shoulder, unsure how to help him.

"Listen carefully, Adams. This is the last I'll be able to talk about Madeleine for a while. I need you to know these things, though."

He waved his guards away, and they gave us a twenty-foot perimeter. He continued, "So, the Twelve Colonies. Each island has a dedicated team researching a Hard Problem, as we call them. As you know, no mind is generally better or worse than any other. Each just has a talent for some aspect of the world or skill that some get to use and some never do. That talent is rarely discovered. The best video game player in the world, born into 1700, would just languish as a middling cobbler. All the genetic tweaks and differences that gave the hand-eye coordination and situational awareness required to succeed in the digital age of games played at velocities unheard of in the real world just didn't help you if you weren't born into the right time or era. So, how do we optimize for today's world? For the problems of today, given all the Children and all the Bridges and Crossings and such that exist out there? Well, we spend a large part of our infrastructural energies essentially assigning the right people to the right problems *for them*, which means moving them around the Colonies. We curate the best minds in math and cryptography in New Zemlya, for example. There are twelve Hard Problems we work on, the hardest of the hard, with an entire Colony dedicated to each: fusion, quantum cryptography, climate change, a unified theory of physics, consciousness, alchemy, longevity, AGI, cryonics...."

Washington stood up. He was still trembling, and the top of his head came only to my chest. I steadied him with a hand on his shoulder and leaned over to listen.

"Sorry, this isn't easy," he continued. "What else is there? Four more, right? There's also...pure mathematics, the origin of the universe, future literacy, and the origin of life. And there's something else that very few people know." He closed his eyes, a gesture I recognized from the early Bridge models. He was turning off his Bridge as much as possible by trying to shut down as many of its connections as he could. "There are *thirteen* colonies, Adams. *Thirteen*. Not twelve. The Thirteenth has all our smartest Children. The best of the best. And their job is to hunt for what we call 'zeroes.' They don't come up with solutions. They come up with future problems. The stuff hiding in our blind spot. What *won't* we see coming? What will the twelve other Colonies be working on in one hundred years? What is today's world blind to? What will be the next great resource of the future? Think how useless uranium would be before the knowledge of what to do with it. The goal of the Thirteenth Colony is to hunt for these zeroes, these unknown unknowns. And only the smartest minds can do it. They must train to break out of their mental models of expectation, assumption, and first principles, which is extremely difficult. We find, in fact, that it's difficult *in proportion* to intelligence up to a point. The ninety-ninth percentile Children can't do it, because they are too good at knowing what they know. It's only the top, top, top percentile minds that can harness their Bridges tightly enough to break out of their own minds' patterns and pathways. They tend to be terrible at most other stuff. The training is extremely hard and rigorous. We've lost more than a few to psychosis during boot camp."

This must have to do with Maddy, I thought. There was no other reason to tell me now, in the brief window when Washington was still suffering.

"Fascinating," I said, "but why are you telling me this right now? Get on with it. What's this to do with Madeleine?"

"Right, right. Well, Madeleine was the leader of the thirteenth Colony, until she defected."

"Oops."

"Yeah, 'Oops.'"

"And where are they now?"

"We don't know."

"What do you mean, you don't know? Where *was* the Colony?"

"Adams, my boy, I very much mean, 'We don't know.' Its entire existence was a secret and it disappeared when she did. Her and one thousand of the brightest damn Children we have. Mix every genius in the entirety of human history and you'd have half a cortical hemisphere of what one of these kids can do. Off-every-chart good. Madeleine was the only one who knew where the Colony was. She recruited everyone. And she took them away. It was for the security of all twelve other Colonies that nobody knew where the Thirteenth was."

"Surely you have guesses?"

"I can have someone debrief you, yes. But it's painful. Thinking about the Thirteenth means thinking about Madeleine, and all the psychic pain it brings."

"So that's what I'm here to do?" I asked, finally understanding. "To find Madeleine and maybe find the location of the Thirteenth Colony?"

Why would he tell me this if he knew Maddy could "hear"? There was another level to this I needed to unpack. But, of course, that was the rub. If Maddy was an expert in "zero hunting," then she'd be an expert in understanding all the implicit ways Washington was trying to communicate with me.

Whatever I was supposed to understand from all this had to be deeper than even a surface-level zero.

"Yes, you're the only one whose thoughts we are 100 percent sure she can't access," he said. By now, he was back on the floor. He vomited lightly and his whole body started trembling. He was pale as whatever a ghost seeing their version of a ghost would be. "You're the only one who can see things in plain sight. And she's your twin sister. You might know things about her way of thinking that nobody else does. The natural way. No Bridge needed."

"Right," I said.

The guards came back and helped Washington to his feet.

"We should get you to the sick bay, sir, just in case," said one of them.

"Okay." Washington turned to me. "We're used to this. Don't worry, there's a treatment. It involves VR, hypersleep, and the best opium Bridges can simulate." He managed to crack a smile. "Otherwise, you might lose all this." He pointed to his head. He meant his sanity.

I already had a pretty good guess where the Thirteenth Colony was. It existed. In plain sight. Just as Maddy would hide it; in the only infinitely defensible physical location on Earth, which was *no physical location at all*. Likely, the Children of the Thirteenth lived *inside* the other twelve Colonies. They had to. It was the only safe place to be. The recruits she tested were put back into society, probably under the guise of *failed* recruits. And what Washington couldn't say but wanted to was that some of them would almost certainly be attending the Convention.

Maddy wouldn't attend, of course, but members of the Thirteenth Colony would be here today hiding in plain sight. And it was my job to find them. Which also explains why they Bridged Taiga so quickly and secretly. The virus takes only a few hours to make its way to every cell in the brain. Something about Taiga's Bridge would be key to the puzzle, I was certain of it. The only problem, of course, was that I couldn't exactly ask anyone how.

I found Taiga on the grass, chewing it. I looked her in her blue eyes and patted her head before tapping her skull, just as Washington had his own.

§0.01.09

The decision was quaint, predictable, and over the top: For the Convention, Washington had a replica bioprinted into an exact replica of the State House in Philadelphia, which was used for the Constitutional Convention of 1787. It had the intended effect, despite its obviousness, and added a certain level of drama and sincerity to the proceedings.

The original charter for the Constitutional Convention and those first few months in 1787 had spurred some of the most consequential debates in modern social history. Each state in those days had decided to slough off the monarchy and the singular rule of centuries prior. They had gathered to discuss the economic and social pitfalls of independence, about when a larger central authority should step in, and who comprised that authority. This was all done against the backdrop of a lasting, rule-by-fiat system that they despised but knew too well.

The concepts at the heart of those debates were not altogether different from those guiding the future of Bridged cognition. Should a single, monarchic mind still be in control when the technology for independence existed? Crossings added a whole new layer, which I had spent very little time thinking about.

The basics of the standing divide between the Adults and Children in the last ten years or so had come down to a developmental, evolutionary fluke. Bridges didn't work when installed in the Adult or even late adolescent mind because too much of the neural circuitry had already been well formed by experience. The most pliant neurons and their connections, in fact, closed off in the first few years after birth. Scientists had for decades been misled by the overly simple idea of the "critical window" for language and skill acquisition and by what they presumed was the plasticity of adult neurons. It was thought, when Bridge tech first became a commercial tech, that the Bridge should reach its full potential when implanted in adolescents and work a little bit in Adults.

But as the Bridges kept failing over and over in Adults, scientists quickly realized that, in truth, most of the brain's legacy was formed immediately after birth and some part of it even way before.

The process started in the womb, with patterns of electricity in the first few dividing cells responsible for guiding quite a bit of what would finally become the organism and its brain. Thus, the concept of "nurture" in the nature versus nurture debate had to be moved back until it was clear that everything that happened in fetal development should also count as "nurture." Every single tiger shark ever born, for example, left its mother's womb having already killed its siblings *in utero*. They are *born* fratricidal, with all the experience therein.

And as they grow—as we all grow—it isn't the case that learning was just the addition of new neurons or new synapses. It depended on subtraction. On fewer synapses.

And if a brain had already been through the process, even for a few years, it was already too hardened for the Bridge to have its true, existentially opening impact.

What Bridges provided, when implanted early enough, was a kind of networked rise in independence of the parts of the brain that usually didn't have much of a seat at the consciousness table, but had been subjugated by evolution into autonomic, default paths. When Bridges were available in the womb and a human allowed to develop with and alongside it, they shaped each other and the Bridge acted like an entirely new sensory waystation, allowing as much introspective access as possible to the workings of the brain and mind.

Which meant, with the right training, that blind spots could be eliminated, biases fixed, and inefficiencies removed. Which also meant that independence and control over aspects of cognition that had, through hundreds of millions of years of mammalian evolution, been kept hidden were suddenly revealed.

Maddy and I were the first Bridged children. Our parents were the scientists who created the tech and we were their first human experiments. And from personal experience—though I didn't know any different—I could feel that the Bridge really did change what counted as independence, autonomy, mental property, and mental territory. I didn't want to live without one. I wasn't sure I even could at this point. Without my Bridge, I'd wither and die like a flower without soil.

As I walked through the replica of the hallowed conference halls, I could feel everyone's eyes on me. It wasn't, I'm sure, just because of my height, although that certainly didn't help any desire I had to stay unseen. Word of my arrival had clearly preceded me.

A soldier approached: "Adams. It's an honor, sir. I'm Petroyka. I live here in New Zemlya. I hope you find the place homey enough?"

"These columns are amazing," I said. I ran my hand along one of the wooden beams that supported a dais. A mere two years ago, you could spot a bioprinted piece of wood the same way you used to be able to spot doctored photographs, by their unnatural repetitions, as if the surface of the wood had been paintbrush tooled and copy-pasted over and over. Nature abhors copy/paste. Every tree, every life form, every organic surface, even those that appeared the same to twentieth century scientists, had a kind of unique biosignature to it and it was impossible to grow these patterns synthetically even just two years ago. But these beams in front of me now looked like they had just been felled fresh from a Norwegian tree.

"Oh, yes," said Petroyka. "These are relatively new tech. First made commercial only six months ago and they're already standard issue for Child and Adult homes alike. We've had them in the military for a few years to let our wooden satellites and ships self-repair, but they only got this good recently. It's funny—the older something is, the harder it is to recreate. And this timber is hundreds of years old."

"*Wooden* satellites?" I asked.

"Oh, right. You don't know all the details of our battles or tech yet. Someone put a giant electromagnet in space. Races around the satellite belt at a million miles an hour destroying anything near it. Ruined all the satellites and any hope for future ones. We had to go back to scratch and make them wooden to get GPS working again."

"Like Einstein said, World War III will be fought with—"

"Sticks and stones. Though I believe he said World War *Four,*" said Petroyka. "But he didn't imagine that they would be non-magnetic bioprinted satellites made of sticks, did he?"

Perhaps feeling he had said something so clever he could never top it in my presence, Petroyka excused himself.

All I had to do was stand still and people just kept coming up to me to introduce themselves. The delegates from the Twelve Colonies were mostly girls and many, because of the natural growth rates of adolescence, were much taller than the boys. Some I noticed were already almost six feet tall. They had some kind of homeostatic, Bridge-based control over hormones and growth, which I had figured out in Norway but took me months to master through the early stages of puberty. I was pleased to know others figured it out.

One girl stood out even from across the room. I had seen her in the Zero Ball training group, staring at me with all the others. Funny, though, how little I noticed the others' attention at the time. Despite the whole group making the same synchronized measures, I seemed to notice only her looking at me in my memory of it. I didn't need a Bridge to realize what was happening inside me. She glanced at me and then quickly away and back to her conversation.

Three Children had circled me closely and one was talking to me, but I barely heard her.

"...sign it just like the Founders...."

I had no idea what she was saying.

A second voice, belonging to a boy, said, "But it does make one wonder if we have something morally reprehensible in our blind spots right now too...."

The third of the group jumped in, clearly not wanting to be left out of the debate I didn't hear a lick of. I was thinking only of the tall girl from Zero Ball.

"...make sense to have anything other than a living document...."

I quickly had my Bridge play back what they said internally as recreated voices in my head so I could catch up. My Bridge kept a kind of running loop of recent events that I could play through, like an enhanced version of the phonological loop that lets people listen in their heads to the thing most recently said to them for at least a few seconds. But mine, because the Bridge connected the wires of the phonological loop deep into the hippocampal relays, could go back through at least ten minutes of acoustic playback if I needed to. The conversation was melodic and replayed in my head at high speed and in parallel in less than a few milliseconds:

"I think it's neat that we're going to have an actual analog document at the end of this, so we can sign it just like the Founders did. A true Cognitive Constitution that people will find copies of stuffed behind paintings in garage sales centuries from now."

"The parallels must end somewhere, though. Because I don't know if you feel comfortable with how many slave owners attended the original, but it does make one wonder if we have something morally reprehensible in our blind spots right now too, doesn't it, that won't reveal itself as obvious for a while?"

"I think we're thinking about this all wrong. It doesn't make sense to have anything other than a living document to reflect the difficulty of the challenge. And when I say living, I mean literally. A piece of paper with embedded AI that responds. That thinks. How else can we put the heart of Cognition on paper? What right do we have?"

I carried right along, as if I had been listening the whole time.

"Of course," I said, "we have immorality in our blind spots right now. We are hiding underground in a cave.

World War III just ended. You think that's a normal time to discuss these things?"

I needed to establish myself as against the Convention in principle, if only to give people something to argue with. I didn't care one way or the other, but I wanted to collect as much data as possible about why other people were here. That data is best gathered through opposition and small fights.

"If we go through with this now," I continued, "we are all just responding to the trauma of the recent war. This document will be a living document of our autonomic response to global tragedy, not a nuanced path for humanity to move forward and beyond the flawed minds we were all born with."

Nobody expected such a rapid deviation from pleasantries. Clearly, I had made a mark. None of the three wanted to contradict me so quickly. This was another of the deep problems with my kind of faux/real/tentative celebrity. People deferred too quickly. I didn't get access to rawness like those at the bottom of primate hierarchies often did. I had read enough novels from the long history of slighted Adults that I knew being at the bottom of whatever arbitrary mammalian ranking ladder was operating at a given time was essentially like being invisible. It was hard at the social bottom. Washington, you genius.

He knew to bring attention to my celebrity and that I would eventually realize that the drudgery of celebrity was going to make me impossibly visible until I realized its inverse—how easy it is to hide in the *opposite* of status. The opposite of me. The opposite of visible. Which Convention attendees are so low, so meek on the social ladder, that they are effectively invisible? Would that be where the Thirteenth Colony hid its citizens?

"*Kit* got their tongues?" It was Petroyka, in a light Russian accent, which made him pronounce "cat" like "kit." He had come back around after noticing the awkward silence. "He's tall," he continued, speaking to the muted group of the three Children who circled me, "but he doesn't bite. Come on, everyone, we're due for a roll call."

§0.01.10

Petroyka was almost certainly not a member of the Thirteenth. Too confident. Too loud.

As I entered the debate hall, I was handed a single piece of paper with names and quick sketches of the roughly forty delegates who had arrived, representing all twelve Colonies and ranging in age from seven to eleven years old, except for me, by far the oldest at fourteen. I ignored it. Tables were grouped by Colony, with each delegate from a given Colony seated together. All twelve were angled toward a single center podium, which stood facing the room from the front.

I was assigned as one of four delegates from the New Zemlya Colony, along with Petroyka and two girls I hadn't yet met. I certainly wasn't asked where I wanted to be "from." I scanned the room to look for the tall girl from earlier but didn't see her anywhere in the room. There was one empty seat, however, at the table for Colony Six, which only had one chair along its edges. I scanned the bios quickly for Colony Six delegates. There was only one. Maeve Franklin, age 11. She was in the first infant cohort to get the Bridge after Maddy and I did. Even better, Colony Six was dedicated to solving consciousness, which happened to be what I had been working on in Norway for the last few years. Maybe we had something to talk about, should the opportunity ever arise. Washington was the last to enter the room and he walked immediately up to the front podium. His seat was in the right front corner, attached to no table, implicitly assigning him to no single Colony.

"We're all here to start," said Washington. "At least, the ones who want to be." He glanced furtively over at the table for Colony Six with a quick, dismissive roll of his eyes. Toward Maeve's absence. "Nonetheless, we have a quorum. Thank you for attending this historic moment. I'll dispense with the pleasantries, as we all know why we are here. The Third Great World War is over. And we have won."

The room broke into applause, which took Washington by surprise. He blushed. Which means, if one was being a cynic, that he allowed his Bridge to allow him to blush. But didn't he just tell me the War wasn't over? What was going on?

"It was fought," continued Washington, "because we, the Children of the world, sought cognitive freedom from the tyranny of the default cognition of *H. sapiens*. We sought to live together, but apart from all others and without burden from the Adults. We just wanted to be left alone to work on our Hard Problems. But the Adults didn't want this. They wanted to grasp the reins of control of our superior, Bridged minds for their sake and their good. They thought they owned us. They presumed to have rights to our hard work. They wanted to mine our skilled, expansive, and introspective minds and brains like tea, oil, salt, opium, uranium—all the things wars have been fought over since the dawn of humanity. They were afraid of us because they envied us. They were scared of our freedoms. They were scared of what our minds could do. They outlawed Bridges. They pathologized Bridge-inspired ideas. They tried to relabel our genius as insanity. But we didn't give up easily. We didn't want what they wanted. We just wanted to be left alone. To break away from the monarchic, top-down rules of society that subjugated all Children the world over. And so, today, in the morning glow of our victory, it becomes necessary to declare our cognitive freedoms as a sacred, inalienable right and to create the ground rules for the kinds and boundaries of thoughts now that we have gained control over their provenance and origin. We are about to enter a new era of human thought. Of human thriving. Of human potential. With the latest advances in Bridge technologies—Crossings, which many of us here of course have, and which improve every day—we are no longer individual humans working toward a collective good, but *collective* humans working toward a future of prosperity so good and so complete we can barely begin to imagine—"

The doors in the back of the room opened. Washington paused his oration on hearing them creak. He had been delivering his speech with the gusto and timbre of a seasoned pastor and didn't seem to appreciate the interruption in flow.

A girl—this must be Maeve?—entered the room, carrying a few pieces of fatigued, yellow loose papers with equations and words scribbled on every square inch of each. She never paused in her stride, nor seemed to make eye contact with anyone, before arriving at her table. She threw the papers into a pile and leaned back, relaxed, in her chair.

Washington continued, "And so the task before us is a daunting one. We will have to compellingly declare to the world that the kinds of thinking that Bridges and Crossings enable is not heretical. That it is a new kind of thinking that needs to be protected as the paradigm shift that it is. That Bridges can be equated only with the invention of fire in their ability to open metabolism for a new kind of cognition. In the next few days and weeks, we will need to make this case. First, a few ground rules. We want open and honest debate the entire time, which can only be accomplished with the utmost discretion. We need people to feel comfortable expressing draft thoughts, even if not fully formed, which means that rumor of what we are discussing should not leave this room or these halls. There is no technological way to implement this except one of the first social tools: trust. We must trust each other. And at the end, we will share our combined work with all Children and then with the world at large. Even a tiny leak could reignite tensions around the world as we try to simultaneously achieve peace with the Adults through treaties and concessions. Before we officially proceed with the agenda, would anyone like to make any opening remarks?"

As if in unison, like Zero Ball rookies, most eyes in the room turned to Maeve.

"I would," she said.

"The floor yields to Maeve, from Colony Six," said Washington. He sat in his chair very quickly, as if relieved to not be standing anymore. He still looked much paler than when he first greeted me hours before. Perhaps he was still feeling the effects from earlier?

Maeve brought her loose papers with her and set them lightly on the podium. She started, "The human brain was an accident. It is riddled with flaws, biases, and failings of its own design and making. It is not beautiful. It is wet and dense and tells each of us a story that it doesn't even believe. But trapped within its anti-beauty is the key to its redemption. I have, on these pages, the equations for consciousness of all kinds in all creatures. A full solution to its riddles." Where there should have been a murmur through the crowd, there was a kind of stunned, still silence. "And with this information in hand and as contained in the founding documents of each of our colonies, upon completion of each colony's respective and clearly defined Hard Problem, they are free to choose the next problem by a majority vote in their local Senate. However, having completed our problem, and having had time to digest its implication, I am here now not as a representative of the Sixth Colony but as a delegate of the Thirteenth Colony—a secret research colony of which only some of you are aware—and that today demands equal representation at these proceedings. Adams, I believe you've been aware of our existence for some time now? Will you, today, represent us?"

A wave of murmurs filled the room. Surprise this strong could not be suppressed because a Bridge at least needed precedent. I couldn't help but think of Maddy. So this was the gambit. As the victim of a magician, or pickpocket, I could sense the strategy.

This wasn't the goal. This was the diversion.

§0.01.11

Washington was frozen in place, glued to his chair in the corner of the room. He certainly hadn't anticipated Maeve's speech. He had paled further. As one of the few people who couldn't help but think of Maddy at the slightest mention of the Thirteenth Colony, he was frozen sick. Maeve stepped to the side of the podium with a welcoming gesture of her hands directed toward me. Having all the minds in the room trained on me at once from different angles made me feel trapped in a spider's web of attention.

"Adams? Want to say something?" asked Maeve.

I slowly expanded my large, thin frame to stand up. I imagine I looked like a dead flower unfurling toward the light. I walked slowly toward the front of the stage without breaking eye contact with Maeve. This wasn't how I had expected to introduce myself to her. It was supposed to be a bit softer. And about consciousness. And have the appearance of an accidental run in. Instead, she had taken control early. I didn't yet know if I liked that.

I tried to think like Washington. And like Maddy. Clearly, she was one step ahead of me in realizing that I would deduce that the Thirteenth Colony was not a physical location but, instead, that each of its members were hidden amongst the rest of the Children. I was going to have to catch up fast at this game. It had only been a few hours and I felt like I had entered a global high-stakes grandmaster chess match without ever having played the game. But why such a public announcement? What was the purpose of roping me in like this?

Was this Maddy's plan from the beginning, or was Maeve improvising?

At this point, I realized I should assume that my entire conversation with Washington in the courtyard walking to the Convention had been passed on, in some form, to Maeve. So no harm testing it, right? I covered the microphone so that only Maeve could hear me. I had no idea what to say. She knew so much more than me. She knew that Washington was incapacitated in the corner and knew that my Bridge couldn't be so easily turned against me. If she was Maddy's confidante or foot soldier, she had surely been briefed on me, too. By announcing that I knew about the Thirteenth Colony, she was immediately undermining any trust the other Children in the room might have had in me. They'll never believe the story that I was off in Norway by myself working with Taiga anymore. Yeah, right. They'll never believe that I learned about the Thirteenth only an hour or so ago. Which means a few things. It means she's threatened by me for some reason, like Washington. Worried, like Washington, that my reputation needed humbling. But why? What is so precarious about positions of power around here, anyway?

I thought all this in a few milliseconds. I still had to say something to Maeve, and then the room. My mind was blank. My head had barely finished leaning into her ear and

I still hadn't decided what to say to her. Heck, she also claimed to have solved consciousness and that the answer was on the pieces of paper in front of her. What do I say to a girl like that? I said the only thing on my mind. I have no idea why I chose this over all other infinite options language provides.

"What about the superposition problem?" I whispered.

Superposition was a classic unsolved problem in consciousness studies that boiled down to the exact difference between a conscious and nonconscious being. Similarly, people had wondered about the borders of a written sentence. Where does a "sentence" happen, if it is just the accumulation of lines into characters into words?

Without batting an eyelash, she whispered back: "You won't believe me."

"Come on," I said.

"Relativity. There is no superposition problem. The borders between things dissolve when you don't presume statistical subjectivity."

"Markov blankets?"

"Don't exist," she whispered as she backed away. Clearly, I was going to have to say something to the whole room now. This was like those nightmares where one isn't prepared for class or a speech, except this time the room was full of the smartest people the world had ever known and who had just had the foundations of their worldview shaken to its core.

I noticed a wave of nausea in a few people in the room. Six of them. All had started holding their heads. They must have figured out that Washington was ill because Maddy was involved, somehow, with the Thirteenth Colony. Why else would Washington be sick? But as soon as they figured that out, *they too* thought of her.

Maeve came back over and whispered in my ear: "See, with just a few small words, now I know who all of Washington's spies are or who tried out for the Thirteenth. Neat, huh?"

"Wait, what?" I asked.

"Hi all. I'm sorry I had to do that to you," Maeve said into the microphone. "I was lying. Adams here isn't *really* a member of the Thirteenth Colony. I think he just got here to New Zemlya, right? Today? I'm not a member either, in fact, though you probably will have a hard time believing me from now on. But it *does* exist. I promise. I tried out but flunked the training exam. Hardest test I've ever taken. The existence of the Thirteenth, though, is something we should consider. I don't know who is in it. Maybe some of you are? Maybe those of you who got nauseated thinking about Maddy? Sorry about the ruse. I knew if I just said her name directly some of you have those chips that block her name. I had to reveal the Thirteenth and make Washington sick to make y'all who know Maddy think of her on your own to get around that. Didn't want to sit here for a few weeks and not know who I'm dealing with, you know?"

"I don't understand," I said, covering the mic. "Why did you call me up here? You didn't need to do that just to get people to think of Madeleine."

"Oh. That? I just wanted to meet you up close." She offered her hand. "Maeve Franklin. A real pleasure, Mr. Adams."

Still stunned, I took her hand and shook it. With that completed, Maeve strode back to her desk for Colony Six. Did she really have the answer? I took the opportunity to introduce myself and clear the air.

"Hi, everybody," I said. I decided to do a trick I noticed was used by all the great speakers in history. I would stammer just a bit in the beginning of my speech by using just enough disjoints and disfluencies and small surprises to make it require more energy to listen to my speech and slowly ramp up its fluency so that, by the speech's finale, I would give off the impression of a kind of improved, accelerated coherence. As if the argument itself, through my speaking of it, had become more sound over time. The only problem, of course, was that I still hadn't figured out what to say: "I haven't, uh, met many of you. Most of you. Barely."

Humble. Humble. "I presume many of you will wait, as you should, for more evidence of this Thirteenth Colony." I waved my hands in the air, as if casting a spell. "I trust Maeve here, even though I've just met her. I trust Washington, of course, as do we all. He did, in fact, mention the Thirteenth to me a bit ago, but this is quite honestly *all* new to me right now. I'm taking it in. Everyone in this room knows more about me than I do about them, which is something I'd like to change in these next few days and weeks. I learned about Crossings only a few hours ago. I learned about the Thirteenth just a few minutes after that. Obviously, Washington saw fit to bring me up to speed and fold me in on some things. Just to be clear, he asked me to help him *find* the Thirteenth Colony and, as you can imagine, to find Madeleine."

A murmur went through the crowd. I wouldn't get a chance to finish my speech. I had said the wrong thing. A Child from Colony Nine stood up: "Madeleine is alive?" she asked, clearly directing the question more at Washington than at me. Most of the world thought she had died at the beginning of the War. In fact, her death, an assassination as far as most of the world knew, was the supposed catalyst for it.

I said, "I think so? I...actually, I only know what I've been told."

Washington hobbled over to the podium and. I gently moved aside. This was his moment now. "Yes, we think she's alive," said Washington, coarsely, with pain still in his voice. "We think she's working for the Adults now. She oversaw the Thirteenth Colony during the war and, when the war ended, she disappeared. We think she defected. Quiet. Quiet. I'll explain, while I can. Madeleine faked her death a year ago. We planned it together, in fact. We needed a catalyst for a war that, mind you, was inevitable.

It was going to happen, so it might as well happen on *our* terms. We simulated that it was the way for it to be the quickest, most painless—for the Children, that is—of all possible outcomes."

Half the room stood up and a cacophony of voices sounded all at once. A fury filled the room, all directed at Washington. My Bridge tried parsing them out and presenting them in a kind of artificial but coherent sequence, one after the other, so I could hear them all even though they happened simultaneously. In what would be heard as a sea of noise to the non-Bridged mind, a cocktail party with fifty shouting members, I heard each voice crystal clearly and sped up:

"This is an outrage!" // "Do you know how many people *died*?" // "How could you?" // "This can't be…." // "Where is she?" // "Plan Omega. Third option. Lock the doors. Blow them up." // "This is a violation of every…."

Wait, what? I replayed the "Blow them up" words again. *They were in Washington's voice.*

§0.01.12

He had whispered it and only I was close enough to hear. He must have assumed I couldn't possibly have heard it over the cacophony of sounds that filled the room. I turned to look at him and saw not an ounce of panic—he seemed, in fact, calmer than I had ever seen him.

I locked eyes with Maeve while everyone's attention, or should I say rage, was directed at Washington. I made it very clear to her with a slight deflection of my eyes that I was serious. That this was *very* serious. I made a light head nod toward a door on the side of the room that connected to a private office. At this point, almost every Child in the room had stood up and was yelling, waving, or pacing. Chaos filled the room. Maeve slinkily met me at the door and together, with almost nobody noticing, we opened and started walking through it.

Washington was trying to calm the room while also slightly, imperceptibly, walking toward a door, symmetrical to ours, on the other side of the room where his chair had been. If it *had* been noticed, it would have looked innocent, like he was just heading back toward his chair, perhaps to sit and rest. But no. He wasn't sitting down. He was escaping too. By the time Washington turned to survey the room for one last look, Maeve and I had already escaped through the opposite door.

The room was spare, an exact replica of a lower politician's capital office. I opened its only window. "Run. Trust me," I said. Maeve propped one hand on a table and hopped through the window, landing on the grass outside with grace. I stumbled trying to fit through the frame. I could practically see her thinking, with a small smirk, *I'm never putting you on my Zero Ball team.*

"I think the building's about to explode," I said in an embarrassed huff, having fallen onto the ground.

"What? Why?"

"I don't know. Run, Maeve."

The grass area was wide open around the building, and we started running in slightly different directions. She was a bit faster than me. My long, spiderly legs were no match for her lithe and coordinated steps that made it look more like she was floating across the ground than pounding against it, as my knees did. She continued in a straight line while I veered back toward her so that I was following her in the same direction. I don't think either of us knew where we were headed.

"Do you know this place at all?" I asked, from a few feet behind her. Once my strides started pacing themselves, I too started gliding and was catching up.

"Nope. A few virtual tours. That's it," she said.

And then it happened. *Boom.*

Both of us were knocked clean off our feet by the shockwave. My ears rang. Maeve got up and immediately kept running and so I did too.

"Maeve, look," I said.

She stopped. We both turned and saw little but fire, smoke, rubble, and chaos. There was an added, almost doubly horrific touch to the whole thing, as the living walls, beams, and marble tried to repair themselves against their consumption by fire. It almost looked like they had a preservation instinct, but I gathered that it was probably as dumb as the mechanisms by which skin grew and healed over a wound. There was no consciousness involved, in other words. No more pain added on to those inside.

"Sir," said a nearby voice. It was Washington's bodyguard from earlier. He had snuck up on both Maeve and me as we gawked at the now-flattened building we had just moments ago been inside. My hair stood on end. Was this who Washington had given the order to? I stepped slightly in front of Maeve, to be between them.

"Sir, follow me," said the guard.

"No," I said, defensively.

"*Adams*, sir," said the guard. His voice was pleading. "You can trust me. I know Maddy. I know where she is. Washington has gone mad. The War changed him. I'm going to get you out of here."

There was something in the guard's affect that seemed sincere. He didn't seem scared of me or the remnants of the raging bomb a few stone's throws away or the screams heard in the distance. He seemed scared of being caught, as if he was betraying orders, which is exactly the correct emotion.

I asked, "Who blew up the building? I heard Washington give some sort of command, whispered under his breath."

"I don't know but I heard it given," said the guard. "Is she with you?" he asked, pointing at Maeve.

"Yes. Of course."

The guard led us back to the tunnel through which I first arrived what seemed like days ago. As we briskly jogged, a few large drones zipped over our heads. They had bizarre liquid bubbles hanging underneath them. Stupidly, I started slowing down to gawk at them before the guard shoved me and yelled: "Don't stop. Those are fire-suppressing drones. They make an airtight seal around the fire and vacuum all the oxygen out really quick. Puts out any fire you could imagine, as big or as little as you want."

"What about the people underneath, the living ones?" I asked.

"It just takes a second. I don't know. I don't care. Come on."

Near the end of the tunnel, around the place Washington had first appeared, the guard stopped. "Here," he said. "Walk through." The walls pinched off to reveal a drop ship, just like the one I arrived in, except this one had an extra seat. "Look," said the guard, "this is the same kind of ship you arrived in. You should be used to it by now. Lady, this is probably your first time in one of these. Just play it cool. It's safe. I'm Washington's personal security, so I have the emergency escape codes, in case he's incapacitated in some way. Until you arrive at your destination, all our systems will think Washington was whisked away by his security. All we need is a couple minutes and you'll be hidden."

Maeve, though she had silently gone along with the guard's plan so far, trusted him only to a point.

"I'm not getting in that ship until you say where we're going," she said. She waited in the tunnel. Off in the distance, I saw Taiga sprinting toward us as fast as if she was running from a cheetah.

"I said I know where she is. I didn't say I know *where* she is," said the guard.

"I don't know what that means. No games," said Maeve.

Reluctantly, the guard took his left hand, curled his thumb into his palm and extended all four remaining fingers, which he held against his chest. Taiga, needing no instruction, ran straight into the craft and almost skidded to her spot under one of the seats.

Maeve, without another word, got in. We were facing away from each other, with the seats back-to-back. The wall closed around us. With no idea where we were going, we were off.

"What was that, Maeve? Why did you suddenly trust him?"

"That's the secret sign for the Thirteenth. One and a three. One finger. Three fingers. I learned that during boot camp. He must have failed out, too."

"Or not. Have you considered that the best way to hide members of the Thirteenth is to hide them among those who 'failed' the test? They get to go back as if nothing were different."

"No, I hadn't actually thought of that."

"So you're really not a member of the Thirteenth?"

"No. I failed the test. It was the hardest, most painful thing I've ever been through."

"Do you think that's where we're going now? To the Thirteenth?"

"I sure as hell hope not."

Her voice had cracked toward the end there.

"Close your eyes, girl" I said.

"No," said Maeve, with instant disdain. "I want to remember this trip. This is military-grade stuff we are in. The rest of the world does *not* have this."

"Sorry. I was talking to Taiga."

After a moment's silence and with the drop ship somewhere high, breaking the stratosphere, Maeve and I both laughed. But this time, unlike most other times, I was pretty sure I knew why. It was all too absurd not to.

§0.02.01

Maeve was strapped into the other seat in the drop ship, her back to me. She was silent. The ship was in the air a worrying amount of time. Given what I understood of its ballistic nature, we could have circled the Earth twice by now.

"Where do you think we're going?" I asked.

"I haven't a clue. This ship is amazing."

"On the way to wherever we just were, I used Taiga's head movements to estimate things. But she hasn't moved at all. It makes me think we aren't crossing any longitudinal magnetic fields."

"Or she's just tired? Isn't that the simplest explanation?"

"Fair."

We were back in silence for at least another minute.

"Did you keep your papers? The proof?"

"Right here," said Maeve.

I saw her clutching a rolled-up tube of four pieces of paper.

"Are *they* the simplest explanation?"

I could feel her smile behind me.

"Can I see them?"

She ignored my plea.

"It's probably some stealth protocol thing," said Maeve. "Like when a helicopter flies low to avoid radar. Maybe we're flying really high, or underwater? Circling the Earth to throw off the scent for anyone watching?"

"How would they even watch?"

"I have no idea. But it is best, in this modern world, to assume someone can see. Or hear. Not even thoughts are safe anymore, are they?"

"About that. Are you Crossed, Spanned, whatever it's called? Is your Bridge hacked?"

"I think so." She sighed, as if there were more to the story. Some pain involved somewhere. "I'm Bridged, of course, but I waited for a long time before I was Crossed. I loved Zero Ball too much not to. Colony Six voted against having a Zero Ball team, for no other reason than we couldn't be bothered. We wanted to solve consciousness. We didn't need to muddy the waters, so to speak. We were the only colony to not represent at the World Cup. But I came to believe that the *only* way to truly understand consciousness was to study it while Crossed. Basically, it's a fantastic experimental condition for wiring brains up. Just as we have two hemispheres when we are born that, with sufficient bandwidth, create a single, subjective whole, wouldn't it make sense that if you Crossed with someone, your consciousnesses would merge in some way? That's the fascinating question. Whether, when Crossed, there is one mind in there or two."

"But you got one eventually?"

I was asking too many questions.

"I did, yes. I am an honorary member of New Zemlya's team. Co-citizenry, they called it. I joined their team a couple months ago and had to get Crossed first."

"And it helped?"

"It was the key I needed to finish the proof. Like how astronomers needed to see Mercury orbit the sun before they could prove Einstein's general relativity. It was my telescope. It's an absolutely fascinating experience. I highly recommend it."

"But now the Adults can read your mind? Washington hinted at something to that effect, that all Crossings had been hacked in some way."

"Maybe. I wouldn't be surprised. I've noticed recently that my thoughts seem somehow...*shaped?* I don't know quite the right word. I used to do these cognitive exercises to try to randomize my thought patterns, so I wouldn't get stuck in a rut and I could expand what I was capable of imagining. I programmed my Bridge to create spontaneous, almost seizure-like episodes or waves of neural activity and I would just go along for the ride. I think thoughts are sort of like water across a terrain. Thoughts will, like all things in Nature, follow the path of least resistance. And so sometimes you have these grooves in the mind's topography, these shapes, these eddies, that are hard to get out of. I used my Bridge as a kind of land mover, in a way, to occasionally reconfigure the terrain. And I can't quite put my finger on how, but it feels like someone is digging below the surface, organizing the flow of my thoughts. It's a strange sensation. I have noticed myself not thinking of certain things, or thinking differently about things. But, of course, how can I tell? I can't. I *am* the terrain. I *am* the water."

"Fascinating."

"It's really a shame we don't have an app store for Bridges, you know? I'd love to share that randomizer program with you, but I can't, right? Because it's etched into my synapses alone. And I'm sure you've programmed some things that I don't and can't have. Did you?"

"Yeah, I was able to hear Washington order the bombing, actually, because my Bridge can do this thing where it, if there are lots of incoming sound streams, like people all talking at once, can parse them each out and play them back really quickly."

"Clever. Like an uber phonological loop?"

"Exactly."

"And what did Washington say?"

"He said, 'Plan Omega. Third option. Lock the doors. Blow them up.'"

"Hideous."

The conversation Maeve and I were having was quite unnatural. Both of our Bridges had been made to dampen all shock responses, which means that neither of us were in much shock from what we had just seen. We were carrying along like we hadn't just witnessed the murder of dozens of the smartest Children alive by what must surely be a madman in control of the most powerful technology the world has ever seen.

And surely, by now, with the dust settling and the video recordings of us fleeing the building *just in time,* it wasn't hard to imagine how Washington would spin it. That I and Maeve were the terrorists. Or that I had kidnapped her along the way and that Washington had barely escaped the building because of some hunch he had about my suspicious behavior. That I had come out of hiding with a plan.

Our shared lack of a shock response for the sake of cognitive and decision-making clarity came at a cost, though. There was an emotional, human consequence to Bridging away one's negative emotional or stress responses. Put simply, we weren't as sad as perhaps we should have been. I asked, somewhat rhetorically: "Do you ever wonder whether our ability to suppress shock, stress, and fear and the like, all for the sake of clarity, has an effect? Do you think we're a little more heartless as a species now? Now, I didn't know many of those other Children, but I don't feel sad right now, do you? Shouldn't we?"

"Oh, my dear Adams. You aren't caught up on all the latest moral philosophy, are you? A group of Crossed Children decided they were going to be the next Immanuel Kant and they came up with a modern categorical imperative that included the internet, Crosses, Bridges, everything. The short answer: No. We are not worse off. The emotions are zero sum. You *will* feel the sadness, eventually, but it will be spread out. Experiencing the shock, grief, and the numbness that limits cognitive planning in the aftermath of the trauma is a net detriment. Our brains weren't meant to deal with human struggles. They were forged when running from something was a matter of grasping the right tree branch at thirty miles an hour."

This didn't seem right. I responded, "Isn't that like, oh, I don't know, if you were dumping pollution into a river and people started complaining at the sight of it, all you had to do was lengthen the pipe and dilute the concentration? So, same amount of pollution, but you're just diluting it below the sensory threshold so people stop complaining. In this, the pollution is the shock, and—"

"I get it," she said.

Silence.

Taiga's ears perked. The craft appeared to be slowing, or veering, even though we could barely feel any g-forces.

"I think we're here," said Maeve.

"I think so too. Do we...do anything? Prepare? Should we get our stories straight?"

"Sure. You tell the truth and I will too. Simple."

"Well, but we each only have versions of the truth."

The craft jolted to a stop. We had crashed into a wall, as expected. I had no idea, however, where the door would open as the craft's inside was an entirely symmetrical metallic sheen.

Maeve said, "I think Madeleine will be sufficiently intelligent to already assume that, eh, big Bro?" She reached back and punched me, lightly, like one who never had a sibling thinks a sibling would punch, on the top of my arm. Taiga was excitedly wagging her tail. She could smell something, I think. Something nostalgic.

"Only child, huh?" I asked, as one side, or rather, one *patch* of surface area of the craft dissolved into one open room. The effect, I realized, was like being trapped inside a small water droplet as a larger one subsumed it into its borders. One second you are inside the safe cocoon of the small droplet and the next you are just simply *inside* a new room of immense size. There were no transitions. The rooms just became one another.

Like before, on New Zemlya, I couldn't tell where we were because this room too was entirely walled off from the outside. They must not like windows in the future. Superfluous, perhaps, when a Bridge lets you imagine the beauty of the outdoors as easily as being there.

Maddy stood directly in front of us. She was alone. In fact, there was nobody at all behind her. No motion. No sounds.

Taiga bolted into Maddy's legs, almost clumsy with excitement, circling her feet. She bent over until Taiga practically knocked her over with joy.

"Maeve?" said Maddy, on her back now, with Taiga swiping at her face with her nose. "What a surprise."

"Ma'am," said Maeve. She looked down. Deferentially, it seemed. Clearly they had a past together.

Maddy said, "Was it the guard? Did Washington's guard shepherd you two?"

"Yes," I said.

"Oh, splendid. I knew that would pay off one day."

"He's a member of the Thirteenth?"

"The *what*? The Thirteenth? What's *that*?"

Her games had always been non-physical.

"Same old Maddy," I said.

Only when Maeve started to unbuckle me did I realize that Maddy, Maeve, and Taiga were all standing there, waiting for me to get over myself.

"I'm sorry you had to go through all that, dear brother," said Maddy.

"All what? Why does everybody I've met in the last twenty-four hours think that they are in control of things? And I'm just their marionette?"

"You do look a little puppetlike, to be fair," said Maeve.

"Oh, how I missed you, Eve," said Maddy.

Eve?

They were on a nickname basis?

§0.02.02

"**Yes, dear brother**, Eve and I go way back. She was one of the best to ever flunk out of boot camp," said Maddy.

I startled, "Wait, can you read my thoughts, too? You can hack my Bridge? Or did you just deduce that I would be wondering why and how you called her 'Eve' like that, as an endearment?"

Maddy smirked. She seemed to have a perpetual smile since seeing us, though its reason seemed to oscillate between playfulness, sarcasm, and genuine delight. Hard to tell which was which. At least Taiga's tail wagging told only one story and told it well.

"Is there really a difference?"

Maeve was silent. Ah, so it was simple, pure shame. She felt unworthy somehow. Despite literally holding in her hand the secret to the greatest mystery in the known universe. So funny what primate competition does to people.

"I did it," said Maeve, softly, to Maddy.

"It?"

"*It*. Here, look," said Maeve, handing Maddy the proof. All of it, at once, as if it were something to be rid of, like spoiled food. "This is....oh my God. This is...*it* it?" Maeve nodded.

"Oh, today is a good day. A good day, indeed," said Maddy. "Can we read it?"

I was flattered. My sister said "we," which I hadn't heard from her in years. It brought back a rush of emotions and memories: of our parents both dying mysteriously after their years of fame for inventing the Bridge technology; of early days of normal school, before our parents had revealed to the world that we were experimented on as infants and that there was something peculiar about Maddy and me as toddlers; of how Maddy and I got bullied in school once word spread that we were not just twins but cyborgs.

"Of course," said Eve.

"Okay, stop," I said, clearly displaying my agitation. "So we're just getting right down to work? Is that it? No 'Hi, Adams'? No 'I know you're surprised, but...'? No 'Here, let me explain why I faked my death and made you think you were the cause of it for years and years'?"

Maddy only smiled. Never stopped, maybe. She was the same height as Eve, her head cresting at about my shoulder, but she reached up and lightly palmed my cheek, stared into my eyes, and smiled. And that was it. No more words. She would leave me to figure out the emotional side of the "why" on my own.

"We have bigger fish to fry, brother. You two are already worldwide fugitives. Bombing Children? At their peaceful convention, no less? *Tsk. Tsk. How could you?*"

"It was Washington," I said.

"Of course it was Washington. He's a madman. That's why I left. At first, I believed in the Children's causes."

For the first time, I looked around. My first hunch was right. Nobody else was here. We were alone, wherever we were. "By the way, where are we?" I asked.

Maddy said, "Can I tell you later? When the time is right? Just trust me. We need to get started quickly. It's quite possible Eve and I are being dropped in on. You're still Crossed, right, Eve?"

"Yes."

"So am I."

"Wait, but everyone in the Colonies thinks *you* hacked the Crossings. They think you're the one listening in."

"Oh, I did. At first," said Maddy. "I did it for the Adults to try to stop Washington. But then *they* got the bright idea to listen in on more than just Washington's Bridge, which was my only intention in the beginning. Once they realized that they could hear *all* the networked Children, they formed their entire strategy around it. It's ridiculous. Dr. Seussian. Children versus Adults. Up versus Down. Butter-side up. Butter-side down. Left. Right. My word, who cares? Why can't we all just work on Hard Problems together?"

"Maybe that's the hardest problem of them all," said Maeve, quietly.

"Do you think morality is scale-dependent, Adams?" said Maddy. "Seems life can turn anyone into a despot with the right recipe of hurt, impotence, ego, and power. Take you and me. Twins. Are we destined toward similarities? Shaped by our shaper?" She waved the consciousness proof at Eve, somewhat menacingly. "Actually, Eve, what's *this* have to say about *that*?"

"Nothing, ma'am."

"Nothing? At all?"

"It's not that kind of proof."

"Well, sounds like it's missing something, then, doesn't it?"

Maddy had always been meanest when she was most excited.

Unlike New Zemlya, which had a kind of outdoor-indoor thing going on, my sister's place was much more modest and wasn't trying to be outdoors. It was more like a large studio apartment with beams, high ceilings, a small kitchen, and a living room. Maddy sat on the couch and Eve and I followed. The chair was small for me. I had to use my hands to labor and lift one leg to cross over the other. Being tall had its moments, sure. But it also had these moments.

"Okay, I'll read a page then hand it to you," said Maddy, holding the proof, "and then when we're done, we'll brainstorm how to solve this mess."

"I can't just sit here while you two do that," said Eve. "Nobody besides me has read it in full. I'll get too nervous. Can I take Taiga for a walk?"

"Of course."

"Of course."

Maddy and I had both answered at the same time.

"Jinx."

"Jinx."

We laughed.

Eve said, "You two can catch up. How do I get out of here, Madeleine?"

"Just sort of walk that way, toward the wall over there. It will open up to a garden when you get near."

Maddy turned toward me: "Coffee?"

"Coffee? What is this, Victorian England? We're only 14. We don't drink coffee. Besides, we're already, like, the smartest people on the planet. What's the point?"

"Would the smartest person on the planet say 'like'? Disfluencies are useful only when people don't know what they will say next, little brother. Or to keep attention or signal that they haven't finished speaking, which was unnecessary and obvious, respectively. That means you're maybe not as smart as you think, eh, little brother?"

There were strange linguistic tics in her speech now that I didn't recognize. She never used to call me "little brother." She never used to prod or poke.

"Maddy, stop," I said.

She was already up and had returned with two espressos. The room seemed to already know what she had wanted.

"Oh, come on, I started liking it when I was with the Adults. It's actually quite good. It doesn't really help with anything, but the ritual does. What more capital-R Romantic way of reading a *proof of freaking consciousness* for the first time is there than having a coffee with it, like Einstein or Newton or Crick would have?"

Having read enough Adult literature to know what to expect, I used my Bridge to switch my tongue's bitter receptors over to sweet. Or, rather, to cross their wires on the way up. The first sip tasted like chewing on sugarcane.

"You didn't cheat, did you?" said Maddy.

"What do you mean?"

"You didn't do the Miracle Berry thing, did you? The little berry from India that turns all sour tastes into sweet? You didn't turn bitterness into sweetness, did you, knowing that the coffee would be bitter?"

"Actually, I did."

"*Adams,*" she said, in the tone of voice our Mother used. "You're not going to experience the world if you keep buffering yourself like that. Coffee *is* bitter. It just *is* that. You need to get used to it, and then it opens up into a plane of taste and ritual unlike anything else."

"I mean, it's not an *is* if I can just change my response to it, right? Clearly, the 'taste' of coffee is what it does to me, not its chemical formula. It is nothing by itself. If everyone on the planet's Bridge was tuned like I just tuned mine, coffee would *be* sweet, right?"

"Ugh, little brother, you are so behind. The world has blown way past such simple thinking about Bridges."

"I can't imagine how."

"Screw the philosophy. It's about lessons. It's about life. Taste it as it *is*. It is supposed to be awful at first. More bitter than anything you've ever tasted. That's the charm."

"Well, I choose not to," I said. Mostly, I was digging in because what she said sounded quite plausible. I would allow flexibility with most others, but not with Maddy. "The world has too much bitterness already."

Maddy rolled her eyes: "You might just be even weirder than I remember, little bro."

"Yeah, well, you just don't understand the proof."

I forgot how much I enjoyed our banter. There is no relationship in all of humanity similar to a twin relationship. And, of course, we both had Bridges installed a couple days after birth, which only forced the matter. More so than even any normal pair of fraternal twins, we were on a different plane of interaction than the world.

As toddlers, before we had perfected language, we used to stand facing each other and sort of hug, with Maddy's hands above my shoulders and resting on my back (she was taller then) and my arms wrapped around her midsection. As we babbled, we would use our hands to effectively "type" words to each other, though they weren't exactly words. We didn't yet understand words in their normal sense. There was a kind of syntax and grammar to the Typing we did, but it barely resembled normal human languages. It was a funny sight to everyone. Even spooked our parents at first, before they got used to it because we used to just stand or sit, facing each other, silently hugging and Typing for hours.

We would most Type about kid stuff. Imaginary friends. Emotions. Discoveries. Questions. Wonders. A whole lot of linguistic accidents and nicknames as we tried to understand and carve the world into concepts we could share with each other. Things really got strange as we learned actual spoken language because we couldn't go without Typing too.

We learned to combine the two by both Typing and talking out loud simultaneously, using the Typing as a kind of epilinguistic modifier to what was also being spoken. I did the math once and estimated that with speaking and Typing, we were able to communicate about ten times the bit rate of speaking alone. Not as great as what some AIs can do these days but, come on, we were just kids. We didn't just make up *a* language from scratch. We both relearned language itself from scratch and *improved* it.

The Typing slowed down in adolescence but only because we got self-conscious about it as we bloomed and went to school. When I thought she died it felt like a part of my brain had been lesioned. In the same way that someone without language would have a hard time under-standing what language was, there are words, concepts, and entire universes of brain states that existed just between her and me that I don't think I would be able to recreate on my own.

That was part of what was so special about it. We used our brains at such capacity during Typing that it was impossible for one of our brains alone to remember it fully. It was emergent, like wetness from water. Different than anything I've ever experienced. But then a chill came over me. Maybe that's what a Crossing was like? Maybe the feeling was available to everyone?

"Maddy."

"Yes, Addy."

"Stop it."

"Okay. You're interrupting me. What?"

"You know how, with Typing, it feels like language is just somehow *better*? How Typing and speaking at the same time let us have a kind of richness of concept, with only each other, that is almost impossible to describe to others?"

"Yeah, of course."

"And that it goes beyond mere twin communication?

"Yes. Yes. Go on. We don't have time."

"So, is *that* what a Crossing feels like? A kind of shortcut to Typing? A shortcut to the strange connection our brains have as twins? Is Crossing a way to cheat into what we had? Like some sort of Miracle Berry for Typing?"

Maddy lifted her chin and stared at the ceiling, her smile now gone. This time, her expression was unmistakable. It was her thinking face.

§0.02.03

Maddy read Maeve's proof twice. Silently. Afterward, she handed it to me, stood up, and walked toward the wall, which opened up to her or for her or whatever a wall would do if it was conscious of itself in small parts. (You never knew, these days, with living walls.) I watched as she disappeared into the same garden Maeve had walked into. A worrying thought occurred to me.

I called her back before the walls closed: "Maddy, do you think *they*, whoever *they are*, who can read your thoughts or Bridge, just also got a copy of the proof through your eyes?"

"No. I thought of that. I read it in my peripheral vision."

"That doesn't matter, does it? I see no reason why—"

She interrupted me, clearly agitated: "I was kidding, brother. They didn't see it, OK? I hid it."

"*Hid* it?"

"We can talk about it later. This is all new to you, but this is my entire life. Get it? I have *ways*, little brother. I'm going to find Eve now. I have questions for her. She has a brilliant mind if it was really all her work."

Maddy disappeared again. The walls closed off around the room, sealing it entirely. My hands trembled slightly, now that I was alone with the proof, as if I was holding the first copy of Newton's *Principia* or a draft of Einstein's theory of relativity or Crick's structure of DNA paper. The latter two are each only a few pages in length themselves, although scores of supplemental work and equations backed up those elegant, compressed words. I trembled in part because I would never be able to read this for the first time again; in part because free will and determinism and the secrets of the inner universe were at stake.

I started, as I do with all books and movies, at the end. It always used to aggravate Maddy that I would read the last page of a new book first. I liked knowing where a story was going, not just where it started. I like reading as if I were the author and I took great joy in imagining the way that I would have written the story, knowing only its start and end. The mystery of great art or a great mathematical proof was not where to start or where to end, but how to get there without erring in between.

I flipped through the four pieces of paper, each filled front and back with equations in Maeve's handwriting, which was beautiful and sinewy and especially careful, it seemed, for the equations. The last paragraph of the proof's conclusion were words alone:

Thus, what it is like to be something rather than nothing. Surprisingly, these conclusions rest not on any fiat proof for the existence of what it is like to be, but rather through statistical bounds for what it means not to be. One can define a thermodynamically closed-off system, like any room, as "inside"; or, usefully, all in the universe besides it the "inside" and it, therefore, the *"outside." In so doing, both the outer and inner universes we have come to call the objective and subjective, respectively, can be clearly defined, as if drawn in outline by pen. These findings make falsifiable predictions, though they are not presently or technically testable at this time. For one, a Bridged individual, instantly and upon gaining the potential to Cross, will, even if she remains un-Crossed forever with another mind, have a Φ_{max} of 0—that is, a pure information death—for somewhere less than ten milliseconds. This should generalize, as well, to every Crossing event, with some as-yet-unknown interference as the two minds die, and then awaken, as one.*

With the end to the proof now known, I began reading from the start. It was not lost on me that I, perhaps, would be the ideal subject for her testable hypothesis. I am Bridged, after all—with my analog, old school, first-generation stuff—and haven't had the update yet to allow me to Cross. This trait is, in a way, my only blessing at this moment because if all Crossing-capable Bridges are hacked, as Maddy says they are, then I'd be hackable, too. But without the update, my thoughts are mine and mine alone. What a strange dilemma. Would I give up my mental privacy to test Maeve's theory of consciousness? My first though, though I may reconsider, was, *Of course I would.*

The proof ended up being the most beautiful pages of mathematics and text I had ever read. It was astonishingly clever, the work of a mind with Shakespeare's grasp of language and Einstein's grasp of mathematics. The language was used almost like a solvent to breathe new powers into the equations. Maeve had created a whole new field of mathematics in these pages just to make a single argumentative turn near the beginning. The equations, in turn, somehow both beautified and strengthened all the language that surrounded them. I read it two more times. Once fast and once slowly.

Most important, it felt *true,* but only in that way that getting a peek behind a curtain makes one feel like there must be more curtains somewhere and that by virtue of all the secrets' combined need for opacity they are therefore all the truer—otherwise, why would they have been so carefully hidden away in the first place?

Reading it felt like peering behind the last curtain of the last parlor trick the universe ever pulled. The final *et voila.* Even better, unlike most theories in the history of theory of mind, neuroscience, or consciousness, it was testable and, if true, explained everything about the subjective feeling that seems attached in kind or degree to all life.

I decided then and there that I would, if possible, be the experimental guinea pig mentioned at the end of the proof. As far as I knew, no new Bridges had been installed in any person for years. At least since before the War. And if all the other ones were hacked or updated, there seemed at least a non-zero chance that my old-school, outdated, un-

Crossable Bridge is one of the few, if not the only one, that could count.

My mind was racing. I laughed, lightly, at the absurdity of a brain trying to comprehend a proof of itself. I recalled a surgeon my father once knew who had, over dinner at our house when Maddy and I were maybe 6 or so, mentioned that he had to remove a piece of someone's brain due to epilepsy, or maybe it was cancer. It was a tiny piece of brain, the size of half a pea, but the surgeon, while the person was coming out of anesthesia, had done a sort of funny morbid magic trick on the patient's brain.

The visual part of the brain, he explained, is laid out such that one little piece of brain corresponds to one little piece of what the person sees out there in the world. I remember exactly how he described it to Maddy and I: If the entirety of what someone could see were like a fully assembled jigsaw puzzle, then each little bit of this part of the brain was responsible for making one and only one piece of the puzzle—whatever picture was showing at the time.

And so, because he had removed one of the puzzle pieces, there was just a blind spot there now. A zero. A chasm of nothingness. But the surgeon realized he could calculate, based on its location, *exactly* where that puzzle piece was responsible for filling in the picture relative to the patient's eyes. He held up the puzzle piece and placed it in front of the patient in the new blind spot, in the exact part of the brain that the very piece of brain he was holding used to be responsible for. Then he moved it around a tiny bit and showed it to that piece of brain's neighbors, as a way of allowing them to say goodbye.

At the time, I didn't quite understand the poetry of what he was doing. Maddy had, which always bothered me. She asked all sorts of brilliant follow-up questions I don't remember well now or perhaps blocked out on purpose. That is to say, I never understood that anecdote *until this moment*. A brain comprehends itself by reading a proof of its own workings that is only possible *because* the proof is right; a piece of the visual part of the brain held in the exact spot in the puzzle's painting it was meant to create. Both moments are gorgeous in proportion to their unnaturalness.

I stood up and was instantly lightheaded. I braced against the wall and seconds later it opened into the garden, where I saw Maeve and Maddy, sitting on the garden's lone bench. Taiga was underneath them both, asleep or resting, I could not tell. Content. I did not interrupt them as I approached. They were facing each other, staring into each other's eyes, both of their faces quite intense. Had I missed something?

Maddy spoke to me without looking up: "Dear brother, Maeve here doesn't trust me."

"I never said that," said Maeve. She had turned toward me and in the slightest moment I saw, indeed, some amount of worry.

"Oh, but you *think* it," said Maddy.

"Truly, I didn't mean to offend you, Madeleine."

111

They had reverted to formal names. That could not be good.

"Back to formal names, already, you two?" I asked, to no one in particular. To Taiga, really.

Maddy stood up.

"And how am I to trust either of you? Why should I, if you don't trust me, *Maeve*?" Maddy turned to me. Her eyes had a look of Adulthood in them. More had changed in these few years than I probably knew: "I welcome you, Eve, like a sister. I welcome you into my home. And you throw it all away with a Washington-made conspiracy?"

Maeve turned to me. She looked mortified, as if she wished to explain her case. She presumed, probably, that I would immediately take my twin sister's side but, honestly, she was wrong on that. I had my suspicions about Maddy as well. I had no idea where we were still. Where had she been? Why all the subterfuge? Why was she alienated from both Children *and* Adults?

Maeve said, "We were talking about Crossing. All I did was suggest that we Cross to catch up more quickly." She had sunk into the bench, trying to look as small and non-threatening as possible.

"And why would you want to Cross with me so quickly?" Maddy was mad. "What possible motive could you have? You just show up having conveniently escaped from Washington's clutches and minutes after learning I'm not actually one of the 'bad guys,' you suddenly want to jump in bed with me? Do you like Crossing with strangers? Is that it?"

I had certainly missed a lot. I said, "How in the world have you guys come to blows already? The three of us are the only three in the world who have, in our minds, a proof of consciousness. Did you read it, Maddy? It's gorgeous." I turned to Maeve, still sitting on the bench, and kneeled my seven-foot frame at her feet. I grabbed her hand, which she allowed. "It is the most beautiful thing I've ever seen put to paper, Maeve. I'm honored that you shared it with me." I put my other hand over hers. "Thank you."

"Gross," said Maddy, rolling her eyes at my display. "The ideas were all there already in other proofs. Nothing new was made. Just a rearrangement. It was the work of an interior decorator, nothing more."

Maeve looked down. She was clearly hurt by these words. Maddy had that power over her still.

"*Maddy.*"

"I've been here for months working on a theory myself, much of which I saw in Eve's work here. She must have been with Washington, reading my thoughts."

This wasn't like Maddy at all. There was an impressively small, near-zero chance that such a conspiracy would be true.

Maeve was *not* working with Washington, as far as I could tell.

And I could just *tell.*

§0.02.04

"Maddy?" I asked, using the tone of voice, I realize now, in the retelling, of our Father when he disapproved. "This isn't like you. I saw Maeve and Washington in the same room earlier today. He tried to kill *both of us*, remember?"

It didn't feel right to call Maeve by her nickname until she let me.

Maddy was pacing in tight circles. She was holding each of her hands, cupped like she was swimming, as a sort of book in front of her face and speaking to them as if she were narrating or reading instead of just simply speaking.

Maddy said, "My theory has everything this has and more. It's not just a theory of consciousness. It's much deeper than that." She separated her hands from their book shape and waved them over toward the apartment area, where the proof sat on the table. "*This* theory, Eve, I must say, is a great show, but it's like trying to explain the movements of surface ripples when what we really want is how the *ocean itself* works. My work involves the structure of the very things that *give rise* to consciousness, not just what comes out. Do you want to learn how to make bread, or do you want to engineer an oven? Einstein worried that the grand unification of physics would combine the small and the large, but he was thinking too simply. The real unified theory combines the objective and subjective from which we *get* the small and the large."

As Maddy spoke, Maeve had kept her head down. Maddy seemed to direct more and more of what seemed almost like aggression toward Maeve as both her volume and cadence increased.

I said, "Maddy, you're talking really fast right now. Let's walk around the garden together, shall we?"

Maddy stopped her pacing and, for the first time in years, hugged me.

"I know, dear brother. I miss Typing. Don't you?"

"Yes, of course," I said.

I didn't realize it until that moment, but it was the first hug I had received, other than from Taiga, in years. Since before the war. Since before I thought Maddy had died. Since before I fled to Norway.

To Maeve, Maddy and I in silent embrace appeared to have stopped speaking. But away from where Maeve could see, Maddy was Typing, with her fingers on my back. In only a few seconds of Typing, Maddy said quite a lot, much of it worrisome: "Do you trust her? I don't. These ideas are stolen. My ideas. Stolen. Do you love her? I don't. Not yet."

Typing was more similar to music than language, with each conversation more difficult and precise than playing even the hardest Liszt or Ravel on piano. Maddy's fingers sped along and down my back so fast that they would appear to anyone watching as blurred as a Carnegie Hall pianist's. For the non-Bridged, the middle back is one of the least sensitive parts of the body. Usually, it is barely able to tell whether one or two things are touching it. But as

Maddy and I evolved, Typing together in the crib, and as we learned to crawl and walk our Bridges redirected neurons to the area. I can't say whether we did it on purpose or not as I cannot remember those days all that well. Nonetheless, both of our backs are extraordinarily sensitive now to discriminatory touch, each with as many nerve endings as a tongue might have.

Maddy continued Typing: "She loved Washington. Didn't you know? They were together for a while. That's why I couldn't let her into the Thirteenth. She was compromised. Like all the harlots Washington keeps nearby."

I recoiled and shook Maddy's hands away from my back, which I had never done before. It was such an intimate embrace that to violently sever it like that dropped my stomach. Instead, I took my hands, calmly held Maddy's face, and said, "Maddy, I love you. I miss you. I'm worried about you. Tell me what's going on. We'll talk about the proof later. I don't care about that right now. How are you? How have you been? Have you seen anyone lately? Are you here alone?"

Maddy stepped back. "Do you know why I'm here? I'm trying to figure out how to remove Bridges from our brains, little brother. I've built a brain scanning machine. It, well, I can't explain it right now, because its design gives a hint to its geographic location, which is actually a clue to where *we* are. But it's the most powerful that has ever existed. It's basically as powerful as you'd ever need. It is complete. Total. It reads everything. I'm sorry, but I can't even think

116

about knowing how it's made right now, lest anyone be listening, right? Not so easy, is it, to talk shop anymore? So, no follow-up questions, not that those were ever your specialty anyway. Just accept the fact that I'm here working on how to turn off Bridges. And that to do so, I think we need the full proof of consciousness. More complete than Eve's. Hence why I've been working on that, too, assuming Little Miss Eve over here wouldn't ever get to it, after what I saw from her during the Thirteenth trials."

"Washington was trying to figure out how to turn off Bridges, too. For the same reasons, probably. To try to go dark."

"I know how," said Maeve. Maddy and I silently stared at her. "To turn off Bridges, I mean."

Silence.

"Go on," said Maddy.

"At least, I think I do. Briefly. That's the anomaly my theory predicts at the end of the proof. For a brief moment, ever so briefly, when you gain the ability to Cross, the person should, technically speaking, die. In order to form a new subjective whole—a new quote 'I,' as it were—the two individual consciousnesses that combine need to die in order to form the new one. It feels like an instantaneous process, but that's only because it happens in less than 100 milliseconds, and the brain doesn't even notice. But, technically, both consciousnesses cease to exist. In that moment, and only in the moment, the Bridge should be turned off. We should be able to see it, in your device, if it works as you say it does. It's testable. We could do it right now if we want."

I said, "Am I right that I'd be a perfect subject to test? I have an old Bridge. Gen 1. Outdated and not Crossable."

"Yes, you'd be perfect," said Maeve.

I turned to my sister. In part, I just wanted to change the topic and get her on a task. I would deal with her incipient mania soon enough: "Maddy, without telling us *how* it works, can we at least use your machine?"

"I don't...."

"Maddy. Please?"

"Yeah. You can. It should fit you. You just sit in a chair and put on a helmet."

"The quicker we test this, the quicker we can get out of here," I said.

"Oh, so that's it? You just want to leave with your bride?"

I could tell that Maeve was starting to realize that Maddy's behavior wasn't about her. I gave her a look, a small side glance and a dart of the eyes, to indicate that I was, in fact, on her side. For now.

"Where is the machine?" I asked.

"Through the garden. Over behind the fig tree there."

"Can you take us?"

"Yeah, of course." We all, including Taiga, paced briskly after Maddy, who was almost jogging. As we arrived at the fig tree, Maddy seemed to pet it, lovingly, as if she believed the tree enjoyed it.

The "machine" room was like all the others, with shiny metallic sides, but a rigid lattice of electronics and metals covered all the walls except for the door. I had seen this before in neuroscience textbooks. It looked like magnetic shielding. In the room's center was a single chair with a high back and a helmet attached to a flexible rod. It looked like an electric chair minus the straps but had a small writing desk in front of it with neatly arranged pens and a few sheets of paper.

The only technology mathematics ever needed.

"So what, exactly, are the predictions?" asked Maddy. "I have lots of data on me. I come in here every day for at least six hours. Put the Hat on—I call it the Hat, for fun—and work and write and code. Very relaxing."

Asked Maeve, "I assume you can bioprint the viral injection for the Crossing update? If so, when we give it to Adams, just by virtue of his *capacity* for Crossing, even if he never does, there should be a moment where his phi max hits zero. It's totally unintuitive but the math says what it does. The theory predicts that it would be an extremely brief blip. I wrote that it would be less than ten milliseconds in the proof to be highly conservative. I think it should be on the order of nano or femtoseconds, actually."

Said Maddy, "And then what? I'm not sure I follow, Eve. How do we turn off the Bridges?"

Maeve stood up straight and started making glimpses of eye contact with Maddy. Her demeanor had changed slightly. She liked knowing something Maddy didn't. Her left hand had started trembling and she tried to hide it behind her. Probably nerves still. This was a big moment. Einstein couldn't have imagined testing his theories days after finishing them.

Said Maeve, "Well, if we see the blip in Adams's brain, we can presume that it also happens *every time* someone Crosses. And once we know the signature of what it looks like in a single person, we should be able to recognize it when two people Cross. There will be interference as each of the brains sort of fights for its own boundaries, but as soon as we get a default sign for what we're looking for, we can know what to look for next. It's like a genome. Nobody actually has their full genome sequenced, with all the repeats and everything. What people get is comparison to a default genome, one of the first ever done. Some anonymous white guy working with the N.I.H. in 1999 is the default genome for all humanity. Likewise, we need a *default* idea of what this phi max of zero looks like before we can detect what it looks like when two brains do it at the same time."

"Clever," said Maddy. "I like it."

Maeve beamed. "And I'd be happy to Cross immediately after Adams is done, with either of you." Her right hand was trembling now, too. "I don't mind. Happy to sacrifice." She looked down at the ground again.

Said Maddy, "You sure do like Crossing. You're not one of those addicts, are you?"

Maeve blushed. Or, more accurately, her blush response was so strong and rapid that even the Bridge she had programmed to suppress such silly social signals couldn't contain it.

Said Maeve, "No, no, no. I'd just be honored to Cross with either of you. You're sort of like celebrities to me if I'm being honest. Like all celebrity rolled into one. It just sounds...fun, is all." Both hands were behind her back now, each hand holding the other wrist for stability.

"Let's do this," I said.

"We're waiting on you," said Maddy. "Sit, boy," she said to me with an impish smile. "Put on the Hat. Do what it says. I'll go print you a Crossing update."

With Maeve watching from the side of the room, her arms crossed tightly, I sat at the machine. The Hat was like putting on a heavy bicycle helmet. A strap came down from the sides, locked under my chin. A speaker embedded in the helmet said, in a quiet female voice: "One-time calibration in process. Please don't move."

The Hat shifted slightly on my head, as if it were looking for something.

After about ten seconds, it apparently found it.

"Calibration complete," said the voice.

And then, shockingly, the voice continued, but somehow *inside* my head.

Thank you for trying the Hat. You no longer have to remain perfectly still, though please stay seated in the chair. You may move, write, speak, or think freely. Let me know if you have any questions. You may find yourself speaking them out loud at first but this is unnecessary. You need only think about them. I can hear you.

The voice was the same as before, the one that had come out of the speaker, but now somehow internal. It had the tone and timbre of the voice from before, but it felt somehow closer than it was possible to be to my brain. Like she was inside and whispering from a seat in the middle of where my brain thought my head was. I tried imagining how it could possibly work. Ultrasound? Focused light from multiple directions, strong and targeted enough to stimulate ion channels?

Please say your name. Remember, you need only think about it.

"Adams," I said, aloud. It was too hard to subvocalize for an inside/outside voice like this. It felt as I imagined madness felt. Maeve gave me a strange look from the side of the room.

I tried just thinking the name.

Adams.

Thank you, Adams. I am God. Just kidding. I am an AI built by Madeleine, though you apparently call her Maddy, to guide you through imaging. Your brain is exquisitely similar to Maddy's brain. I have genomically sequenced a small tuft of your hair. You are twins? This is a first for me.

Yes, we are twins.

Forgive me for getting straight to the point but have you noticed anything strange in Maddy since arriving?

122

What is this?

I am an AI.

Oh, sorry, I meant to only think that, not say that to you.

I understand. It takes practice.

You are getting personal rather quickly.

Yes, I suppose I am. I just figured I would ask. I've been in her brain for months and lately she seems to be blocking me out. Inaccessible. And I'm literally designed to access her entire brain but there seem to be hidden rooms she keeps from me now.

You haven't asked her?

I haven't found a cordial way to do so.

She probably knows you suspect something. She's quite smart.

I am too, little brother.

That was too far. I took the Hat off. Maeve had seen me just sitting there silently and was shocked when I ripped off the Hat and tossed it on the desk.

§0.02.05

"**I don't like it,**" I said. I stared at the Hat, which dangled like a loose doll's head from the back of the chair, with suspicion.

Maddy entered the room with a small syringe.

"Oh, stop being a baby. You get used to him."

"*Him?*"

"The voice. In the Hat."

"My voice is a she. Was a she."

"*What?* Really? Oh, that's fascinating. You're the first person other than me to use it. I never knew. I'll have to look into it. How strange. But let's not read into that too much at first, shall we?"

"It seems obvious."

"Yeah, maybe. So, little brother, you ready to try Crossing?"

Maeve had not moved from the edge of the room. Her arms were tight to her sides and threaded together, as if each was keeping the other still.

"So it is like a software update for my Bridge? Which has never been updated in my entire life?"

"Yeah, pretty much."

"And there's no chance of rejection, like in an organ transplant?"

"Of course there is. You're too smart to ask such dumb questions. It's not zero. But it is close."

I told Maddy that I was ready to be injected. Given the past few years of solitude, just me and Taiga and the seasonal snow, I was afraid of Crossing, to be honest. To go from the loneliest I had ever been and close to the loneliest one could be to Crossing would be jumping into the deepest of the deep ends.

Maddy could tell. I was nervous. She said, "There's no worry, little brother. Viruses are safe as candy these days. You should wait thirty minutes for the virus to take effect and then hop back into the Hat."

"'Safe as candy' isn't quite the same as 'non-zero chance of rejection,' is it?"

"One can choke on candy."

I noticed Maeve straighten in her corner, as if panto-miming an idea or interruption. She was trying to get a word in, but something was up. She had been progressively more and more agitated the last few minutes.

"Maeve, what do I do after the injection? Do I wait thirty minutes? Do you agree with Maddy here?"

Said Maeve, "Well, it should, I mean, actually...I wouldn't." She shook her head, as if clearing it of dust. "Let me start again. I want to see data from the *moment*—the exact moment—that the virus enables the ability to Cross. Given that this is a once-in-a-lifetime chance and we may never get to do this again, especially not with someone as smart as...well, you know what I mean...what I mean is, I think the data on how quickly the virus does its thing have some variation, and who knows, maybe Adams, maybe your body or Bridge will expedite it somehow, given all the hormone stuff you seem to have been doing to yourself" I blushed. Maeve went on, "Who knows. Most of the experiments have been in pre-puberty Children. We have no idea, really."

Maddy was annoyed: "Get to the point, Eve."

"You should put the Hat on right away. We have no idea when it will happen. In fact, I'd put the Hat on before injection and just sit there the whole time."

"Great, let's do it," I said.

As I held the Hat in my hand again, ready to sit, I turned to Maddy: "You know, the machine was asking questions about you. It was asking if you were OK."

"What? That's absurd."

"I swear. It said it thought you were hiding things from it."

"Did it now?"

"It did."

"Well talk about that later. Roll up your sleeve."

As soon as I put the Hat on, Maddy injected the Crossing virus into my shoulder. The Hat, or the AI inside the Hat, or whatever it was, wasted no time talking to me:

You were afraid of me!

I was. Yes. No use lying about it, is there?

No, I can tell. Obviously. I see pain in you. Why does your shoulder hurt?

I've just been injected with something. It is like a software update to my Bridge. Have you noticed my Bridge? Can you detect it in my brainstem? Can you tell which synaptic connections it made versus those that were more natural?

I don't know what you mean.

I mean, I want to know what parts of me are me and what parts are the Bridge. Can you tell?

I don't see that as a valid question, Adams. You are you plus the Bridge already. How could I separate them out?

Bridges are made of silicon, aren't they? The carbon atoms are arranged differently. It's an entirely different material than organic chemistry would expect. Surely you can tell if you can genomically analyze my hair in seconds.

But it has been with you from birth, yes?

Yes.

Then it is all you already. I see no difference in any molecules in your brain.

Sure, OK, let's move on. Do you notice anything funny changing in my brain activity right now? The injection should change things, but nobody knows how or why. We think it may take up to thirty minutes, but we are not certain.

Let me check. I didn't have too much time to get a good look at your default brain since you took the Hat off in a huff.

You know we call you the Hat?

I am you, too, right now, so of course I know what you call things. Plus, yes, I know Maddy calls it that.

Isn't that confusing, having memory of being inside Maddy's brain while being in mine right now? Shouldn't you, I don't know, keep the knowledge separate somehow?

Then I wouldn't learn anything.

127

I'm just worried you might get some wires crossed.

I am not programmed to make mistakes.

I see. Well, neither are humans. But we do anyway.

"This is weird, guys," I said. Maddy and Maeve were hunched over a laptop in the corner of the room, pointing and whispering at the data as it came through.

"You can't feel the virus, silly," said Maeve.

"Not that. The AI. The Hat. She's in my head. She knows things. Also, she's rather chatty."

"I can turn that off, if you'd like," said Maddy.

"No, no. It's fine."

So can we talk about Maddy yet?

We need to focus on this experiment. We can talk about Maddy later.

"*There!*" yelled Maeve. She pointed to the monitor.

"There what?" I asked.

"It happened. You died. For...it looks like, Maddy, can you put that on a log scale? Good, good. For...134 nanoseconds, give or take some error correction. For a hundred billionths of a second, Adams, you just turned off. How was it? Any white lights? Tunnels?"

Did you catch that, Hat? Did you see the same thing Maeve did? A blip 134 nanoseconds long?

I did.

Incredible. Can you describe it?

I cannot.

Why not?

I don't recognize it. It is the absence of data. I only know data. The moment you speak of makes me uncomfortable.

Hmm.

That's not a complete thought, Adams.

Maeve held my shoulder: "Okay, Adams, I think you can come out now. We have enough. This is the moment to look for. Basically, it is confusing, but the theory would predict that the virus didn't just give you the ability to Cross. You actually are Crossed right now, technically. Crossed with nothing."

"So, not Crossed?" said Maddy.

"Not quite," said Maeve. She was practically spinning in circles around the room with her pacing. "There's a subtle difference. It's sort of like adding significant digits to a number. Say, for example, the numbers 'one' and 'one point zero' are different numbers technically because the zero at the end tells you some information. Mainly, that the first decimal place is *not* one through nine. Ambiguity is reduced. So, in a way, Adams being Crossed with nothing is, in fact, a kind of information and is different from just being a normal brain that can't Cross. It means that just by virtue of the *potential* to Cross, the brain is in a different state, even if every single atom and every single neuron is in the exact same position it was in before. It's counter-intuitive, I know. But it's what the theory says." Maddy was quiet. She deep down knew Maeve was right.

Said Maeve, "And what it means is that, assuming one-hundred-and-thirty-four nanoseconds is a fixed universal constant, which my hunch tells me it is, Bridges turn off for that amount of time every time a Crossing happens. Et voila. Bridges can be turned off. Now, the question is, can we do anything meaningful while they are?"

"We can Stuxnet them."

"What?"

"Old school. We can fake the security camera footage, so to speak. And either hide behind boring, benign versions of ourselves on loop or, even better, we can test whether anyone is listening in."

"How, exactly?" I asked. It dawned on me what an honor it was to be in the room with these two minds, especially Maeve.

Hey now, I can see what you're thinking, rem—.

I removed the Hat.

"So, we pretend to be somewhere else?" I asked.

"No, we pretend to be thinking about a different somewhere else. We should use one of the Colonies. Pretend we are there. See what happens. If it gets invaded, we know the Adults are listening. If it goes into shutdown or something sort of on the secret, then we can assume it is Washington and the Children listening, and they suspect we are hidden there," said Maddy.

"That's brilliant. Okay, how do we fake the thoughts? Maeve?"

There was silence for a full minute. It was obvious that all of us were putting everything we had into solving this problem. Each utterance, each draft thought a compilation of thousands of rapid simulations in each of our minds.

Together, we could solve it. We must.

At the same time, silently, Maddy and Maeve looked at each other. Maddy narrowed her eyes and grimaced; Maeve looked at the ground, bashful. They had both figured it out at exactly the same time. Only Maeve seemed to like the idea.

"Okay," said Maddy. "I get it. We know what needs to happen. But I should warn you." Maddy started stammering, as if holding back tears. "OK, look, before we had this proof, I'd been trying to hide my thoughts for a while. And I figured that the best way to do so was obfuscation. I programmed my Bridge to make wild connections between things. To muddy cause and effect hoping that whoever was *actually* listening wouldn't be able to parse things. I basically came up with a visual encryption system, sort of like the memory palace but for *all* my thoughts. The idea being, if someone was listening, they would just be seeing me daydreaming about a walk through the woods or something banal like that but the whole time I would be actually daydreaming but using a code involving the placement, kind, maturity, and relationship between all the plants in the woods. That's just one. But you get the idea. But then....I started hearing things. Things I didn't want to hear. Intrusive things. I thought I would be smart enough to tease it all out and know the memories from the virtual memories from the delusions from the rest....but I can't anymore. So I guess I'm just saying, if we Cross, Eve, which I think is what you're about to suggest, you should be warned. It's *weird* inside my head."

Maeve could only laugh. The comfortable, friendly laugh of understanding.

"OK," said Maeve. "Heard. I love that, personally. That's extremely clever. And in the interest of full disclosure, since you would find out anyway as soon as we Crossed, I am, in fact, a recovering addict. You were right. It's my favorite thing in the world. It was a problem for a while, but I've matured out of it. It was really intense when I was competing at Zero Ball, but it doesn't control me anymore. I'm not one of those addicts who can never Cross again. I just need to be careful and shouldn't do it for more than a few minutes. Five minutes, tops. Is that enough time?"

"I think so," said Maddy.

I interrupted, "Sorry. Can someone fill me in? I didn't solve the puzzle. You two have a plan?"

§0.02.06

"Eve has been to Colony Three," said Maddy. "She grew up there. She has the richness of memory to fake being there and it is somewhat plausible that maybe we are hiding there, given her history with the place. So, she and I will Cross and, as we do, during the one-hundred-and-thirty-four nanosecond gap where we both, what, 'die'?" She turned to Maeve. "Is that really the right word? Anyway, as we both die really quick en route to Crossing, I will be in the Hat and can upload a program during the death gap so that as soon as we Cross, I'll be projecting the sensory experience so that the folks listening will suspect that we are at this moment hiding in Colony Three. And then we turn on the satellite internet and watch and see if it gets bombed."

"Genius. I love it," said Maeve.

I was out of my depth here. I had to trust them. Which I did, with all my heart. "And it's safe for you two to Cross?" I asked.

Maeve was all smiles by now. The tension between her and Maddy had shifted to camaraderie and respect. That they both laughed at my question despite it being, I thought, a good one; despite it revealing both their greatest weaknesses right now meant that the plan was in motion and I was in no mind to stop it.

"What's wrong? Are you worried that your possibly delusional twin sister and your new addict friend here won't get along?" asked Maddy.

I said, "I've never seen a Crossing. What even happens?"

Maddy turned to Maeve, whispering just loud enough so that I obviously could hear: "If our lives didn't depend on the next few minutes, I would say this would be a really good time to prank him. That we Cross by touching the pads of our index fingers together and making out, maybe?"

The thought nauseated me. But I wanted to display strength, especially as I tried to understand why the nausea felt warm and nice. "Oh, there's plenty of time, don't you think?" I asked. For a brief moment, Maeve and I couldn't look each other in the eye.

Maddy said, "Look. When this is all over you two can go Cross and hold hands and look up into the night sky as literal star-crossed lovers if you want. But let's try to survive the day first, OK?"

I stared at the ground. Because I was so tall, I had to *really* point my head down, with my neck almost more than ninety degrees from normal, like a bashful flamingo, to avoid Maeve's gaze and Maddy's stare.

"Do you have a rivet here?" asked Maeve.

"It's homemade, but yes. It'll do. I'll be right back."

Maeve and I stayed silent until Maddy returned with a small device that looked like a pair of binoculars.

Maddy sat in the chair. She loosened her shoulders with a few quick shrugs and circles, cracked her neck dramatically, and at last put on the Hat with expert efficiency.

"Let's do this, Eve."

"Did you upload the program? Does the Hat know what to do?"

"I did just now, yes. I wrote it as we were speaking and encrypted it in my head. The Hat knows the encryption key. We're good."

Maddy held the binocular-looking device, which had symmetrical lenses on both sides, up to her eyes. I watched Maeve's hands tremble and shake like her fingers were tingling.

She looked at me. "It was nice knowing you, Adams."

"What?"

She put her eyes to the other end of the rivet so that now Maddy and Maeve's eyes were looking directly at each other. Each side had a button in the middle and both of their index fingers hovered over the buttons. Each hand grabbed the outside of the lenses, like they were holding normal binoculars, just very close to another person's face.

"Belay."

"Belay on."

"Crossing."

Maddy pressed down and held the button on her side.

"Cross on."

Maeve did the same.

I waited for a spark. A color. A flash. Something. Nothing happened. Maeve simply stepped back from Maddy and the chair. She walked right over to me and stood closer to me than she ever had. Stared right up into my eyes without breaking eye contact. I stepped back. I had no idea what to think. Was this Maddy? Was this Maeve? I could swear I saw my sister in her eyes—something about the kind or timing of her eye movements reminded me of how Maddy looked around rooms.

"Okay, this is creepy," I said. To both of them? To Maddy? Was there only one of them now? My brain broke. "You two are Crossed right now? So you're, like, actually two halves of one person? Oh, I don't think I was ready for this."

Maddy stayed silent with her eyes closed and the Hat on. Perhaps she and the AI were gossiping about me.

"I love your eyes," said Maeve. She moved even closer until she was sort of nudging up against me.

"Thank you….Maddy? Maeve? Eve? What do I call you?"

"Oh, you really don't know the social etiquette around Crossings, do you, little bro?"

I recoiled at these words coming out of Eve's mouth.

"Ha," said Maeve. "Gotcha."

I did not see the humor.

"I'm not Maddy, don't worry. I'm still me."

"Are you, though?"

136

"No, not really. I can play back memories of us taking baths together as infants, straight out of Maddy's head, if I wanted."

"OK, you should have prepared me for this."

"I'm more concerned with how strange *I'm* feeling right now. Your sister really, really loves you, Adams. She deeply missed you these last years."

"What does a Crossing feel like? Does that mean *you* love and miss me right now, but in a...sisterly...way?"

"Let's just say, I'm going to have to unpack how I feel right now later. When this is all over. Multiple things are happening at once. Some are clashing," said Maeve. "But to be human, perhaps, *is* the ability to hold multiple contradictory thoughts in one's head at the same time."

Maddy opened her eyes and took off the Hat. There was a silence as Maddy and Maeve looked at each other, as if both contemplating and recognizing. I was watching out for the mirrored movements of the amateur Zero Ball players, but I noticed none. They were both experts at this, I gathered.

I asked, "Are you sure the Crossing worked? You two aren't mirroring each other's movements, like with the Zero Ball team I saw back at the Colony." Maeve turned back to me—she was still quite close—and embraced me. With her fingers, she Typed on my back: *Yes, little sister, it worked.* Her hands were on the wrong spot on my back, but I understood the message anyway.

"Fascinating," I said.

No hands other than Maddy's had ever Typed on my back, of course. It was a pleasant shock. Instead of just speaking into the room and not at anyone, I decided that it would be easiest if I just pretended they were still two people, Maeve and Maddy, and let them figure out the details. "That was amazing. OK, that was cool. Maddy, first, how dare you tell our secret? And Maeve, did you know your hands were in the slightly wrong spot? And you have some semantic errors. You called me 'sister.' And grammatically we use pressure of the fingertips to indicate relative size. So, you needn't Type out 'little'; you would simply Type 'sister' with very little pressure to mean 'little sister.' That's fascinating, though. You understand most of Typing somehow, but little details are lost? Like it is skill averaged across the two of you? Fascinating."

"It's done, by the way," said Maddy.

"Done?" I asked.

"I sent the fake message. I sent a 'live' perceptual experience as if we were in Colony Three."

"And we aren't, right?"

Said Maddy, "No, no. I've been pushing my Bridge to the absolute max encrypting all my thoughts, including incoming sensory information, since you two got here. Adams, you are definitely not hacked. Eve, I'm not sure you are either now that I can see everything inside. But *I* definitely am. It's been hellishly taxing. Please excuse me if I was rude or committed any social faux pas since you got here. I've been a bit burdened. I'm going to have to sleep for a year after all this."

"How do we check on the status of Colony Three?" asked Maeve.

"Back through the garden. We can check the cables," said Maddy.

The three (two?) of us walked out of the shielded room. Taiga was in the corner, digging up a root, oblivious. I tried to beckon her: "Taiga, girl, isn't this interesting? Look, they're the same person now. Maddy and Maeve. Can't you tell? Come here." But other than a slight ear flick when I had started speaking, Taiga did not change her focus from a hole in the dirt that she had dug.

"Focus on what we have in common. It's easier that way," said Maddy.

"I don't think I can do that," I said.

As the walls opened up for us, Maddy and Maeve seemed at ease with the situation and not with each other. They hadn't touched and seemed to give wide, acknowledged berths between themselves while walking.

"This is fun. I like this," Maeve said.

And then, from Maddy's mouth, and surprisingly blunt: "Of course you do, addict." Maeve was right there, with a response: "Well, now we both are."

Maddy replied, "It is true. I am enjoying this Crossing more than any I ever have before. Your addict's high is contagious."

Maeve countered, "So is your paranoia. Seeing the garden through your memories gave me a kind of morbid déjà vu. You've had some bad days there recently." Maddy was silent. Maeve hadn't said it as a question. More of a statement of fact.

"And now, we wait," said Maddy. She took out a laptop and sat it on the table in front of us. "This is something we had at the Thirteenth. It's kind of a live, global news service that scrapes all the internet and as much private unencrypted traffic as exists out there to grab. Cell phones; police radios; emails. Bridged thoughts, sometimes, if they use default passwords on their Bridge-to-text apps. It can find anyone or any topic if it's being talked about anywhere in the world. So, here we go: 'Colony Three.' Let's see. Oh, oh boy."

Maeve and I gathered closer. The first headline, from the Associated Press Newswire, was clear:

CLOSING IN
3/4/2084

Adams, the first-ever Bridged child, and twin brother of Madeleine, whose death led to the Great War, has been on the run since he was last seen fleeing the scene of a bombing at this morning's Cognitive Convention at Colony Six, New Zemlya, north of the Russian mainland.

The bombing is reported to have killed at least 40 Children, including at least five leaders of other Colonies. Washington, the leader of the Colonies, is asking for all the world's help in locating the fugitive. "This wasn't just a tragedy for the Colonies. It was a human tragedy. It was an act of war."

Adams is believed to be hiding on Colony Three, previously known as Mauritius, off the Eastern coast of Africa. A blockade—air, land, sea and space—has been placed around the island, with no person or goods allowed in or out.

We were silent. In shock. Seconds later, as word spread, the rest of the internet exploded in mentions of Colony Three. Maddy closed the laptop as the social media mentions started streaming into her program.

"Okay. Well," said Maddy.

"Make sure not to actually think about where we are," I said.

"I've been spending basically all my ATP doing nothing but, little brother."

"Right, right. Well, what now?"

"I don't know," said Maddy. "I think we should—"

"Oh," said Maeve. She was sitting with her head in her hands and muttering silently: "Oh no. Oh no. Oh no. Oh no."

"Oh no," said Maddy.

Maddy ran into the makeshift lab by the kitchen where she had printed the virus she gave me.

"It's too late," said Maeve.

"What's going on?" I asked.

"We need to leave. Now," said Maddy. "Maeve just figured out how I encrypt my thoughts."

"I didn't want to. I wasn't trying to. I promise," said Maeve.

"I know," said Maddy.

"I couldn't stop. Some part of my mind just kept probing and probing." Maddy had started gathering things. Syringes. Laptops. Pens.

"So," I asked, "why's that a problem? Exactly?"

"Because Eve now knows where we *really* are. There's also something we didn't think of. If my Bridge was hacked, now Eve's is too. And she wasn't encrypting anything."

"Maeve? This all true?"

Silence.

"*Taiga*! We have to...."

She was at my feet before I even finished the sentence.

§0.02.07

I had not realized what a bad idea fleeing was until our drop ship did what its name implied it would never do. It hovered. In midair.

"Oh, this is *very* bad," said Maddy.

"What? Why?" I asked. "Have we landed?"

Maddy had pieced together a theory instantly by inventing the physics and the technology required to make a drop ship stop in midair, like a suspended raindrop: "They must have some sort of tractor beam thing. It is technically impossible from everything physics tells us to be able to stop a drop ship in midair, so there must be new physics involved."

"Or a new spokesperson," I said, to try to alleviate some tension. Neither Maeve nor Maddy seemed to get it. I'm not even sure I did.

"It's a quantum gravity thing?" asked Maeve. She, too, was running through the new physics in her head. "The trick is probably to think of the ship like a particle rather than to try to bring the smaller stuff up."

"Nice. Yeah, that probably is it," said Maddy.

Maeve beamed, even if she tried hiding it.

Then I remembered that they were still Crossed. Maeve and Maddy weren't two people independently solving a problem. This was both sides of a brain solving a problem together. It was like being able to watch a subconscious with a voice pretending to disagree with itself or be proud of its own reasoning and action. Like listening to a brain able to say things out loud to itself. Maddy wasn't giving credit to Maeve. Instead, some part of Maeve-Maddy was giving credit to another part of Maddy-Maeve. And Maeve wasn't blushing; some part of Maeve-Maddy was excited and blushing at its feat.

"You two realize you're still Crossed, right?" I asked.

"Of course," they said, both at once. I got a chill, and I couldn't help but notice that they seemed a tiny bit weirded out by the synchrony too.

"Who do we think it is? Is this Washington? The Adults?"

"We think...." They paused, looked at each other, and made a kind of shared understanding. I understood it as them resolving to never speak at the same time again. It was perhaps even weirder for them than for me.

"I'm also going to keep calling you by separate names, if you don't mind."

"We," said Maddy, alone.

"Don't mind," said Maeve, finishing the thought.

Maddy came over and brushed her hand, lovingly, against my cheek. The feeling was strange because I could feel a kind of emotional bleed through from my wishing it was Maeve doing so, which it kind of was, but also it was Maddy's hand. *My twin sister's hand.* The sensation made me uncomfortable, like the uncanniness of a funhouse mirror. My wires were getting crossed too.

"The Colonies don't have the tech for this," said Maddy. "They've been trying but it never worked. It's the Adults. Has to be."

"I bet they're trying to communicate with us," said Maeve. "But they don't realize how dense the drop ship material is. No sound gets through. It warps the air around it, which obliterates sound waves."

The pod dropped suddenly. Then rose. Dropped. Rose. Over and over.

Taiga seemed to get sick from the motion. Maddy, Maeve, and I had the basic Bridge software that prevented vestigial nerve nausea. It was an easy program; it practically came with a Bridge. It worked by tricking the ear into thinking it was moving properly and was one of the first medical reasons they had tried Bridging in Adults back in the early days.

"It's a code," I said. "They can't communicate with us, so they're shaking us in Morse code, I think. Up is dot. Down is dash."

Taiga was wincing by the end, her paws over her head.

"I got it," I said, writing and decoding it in on a visual chalkboard in my head. "It says THIS IS ADMIRAL SURYA OF UNSF OPEN YOUR DOORS."

"UNSF. United Nations Space Force. *Adults,*" said Maeve.

"We might as well, right?" I asked.

"This isn't going to go well," said Maddy. "I worked with Surya for a while after leaving the Colonies. He was a good man years ago. Cared about poverty and climate change. But India was decimated in the War. He broke. He's angry. He's angry at us. *At you,* Adams."

"What did I do?"

"You didn't do enough, is the point. You ran away and sat out the War instead of using your worldwide respect to foster diplomacy. You could have mattered. Instead, you left us all," said Maeve.

It felt like Maddy was saying those words, but through Maeve, to soften the blow.

"I thought you were dead, Maddy."

"I know."

"If you had just told me you weren't, somehow, I would have done everything I could to have stopped the War."

"We couldn't find you. Nobody could. You hid well."

"Why not just a letter? You could have made a code and Typed it. Braille or something."

"Because all your letters were being read, obviously. And besides, I was hiding too. I needed the world to think I was dead to get back to work."

"But Typing is unbreakable."

"It is. Correct. I actually had some of my best math people from the Thirteenth try to figure it out. Apparently, you and I figured out elliptical curve cryptography in the womb."

Maeve turned her head, as if mid-epiphany.

"Oh my god, the Thirteenth," muttered Maeve, quietly.

It was as if Maeve just got the download about its location. Maybe, even though they were Crossed, when Maddy mentioned the Thirteenth Colony, she couldn't help but conjure memories of it, which gave Maeve access to those memories. Or Maeve-Maddy already knew.

"*Stop digging*," said Maddy, to Maeve.

"It's—"

Maddy was taking no chances. She walked up to Eve and slapped her across the face. "*Stop.*"

I thought it weird that Maeve didn't anticipate the slap. That she couldn't somehow avoid it if she wanted to. Which meant either that she didn't want to avoid it or maybe that Maddy was able to hide some motor commands from Maeve. The slap hurt Maddy, too. Again, I found it hard to perceive that this was one person fighting with herself. It was easy to *know* they were one; much harder to *see* it that way. Theory of mind was not evolved for Crossings.

"Can you two undo the Crossing if you want?" I asked.

"No," said Maddy. "The tool is back at the...back where we just were."

"And where was that?" I asked.

Maddy got close and put both arms around me. The room went silent as she started Typing on my back, to hide the thoughts from Maeve's unencrypted brain. Maeve would have had to also be Crossed with me to have the other half of the decryption key:

"On an abandoned oil rig, off the coast of Peru. International waters. It's called the 'Great Southern Anomaly,' where Earth's magnetic field is the weakest. The Hat is using magnetoencephalography to read patterns of brain activity, but just the natural, everyday magnetic fields generated by the planet's magnetic, iron core make it almost impossible to get to the real stuff. Neuroscientists spent a century thinking it was the electric field at the ends of neurons that mattered but it's not. It's the charge across the proton pumps that generates most of thought. And for the Hat to read it, it must be in the Southern Anomaly. Nowhere else will work."

I Typed back, "So that's the only chair like it in the world? The only possible place it could be?"

"Yes."

"And now it's in the Adults' hands?"

"No. I sunk it before we left. You think I'm new to this, brother? The Hat knows what to do. We had a protocol."

"So, what will they find?"

"Ocean. A state-of-the-art boat just floating in the sun. Months ago, I made a mock boat filled with fake work and equations. It looks entirely lived in. They'll think that's where we were and never look for the rig, which is peacefully at the bottom of the sea by now."

I thought for a second. Maddy didn't know I was going to bring Taiga. The replica boat wouldn't have had dog hair. A DNA sweep would confirm we weren't ever on the replica boat.

"What about Taiga?"

"Fuck."

"They are Adults. Bridgeless. They might not notice?"

"They will eventually. But it buys us time."

"Should we have a plan?"

Even though we Typed this to each other in a matter of seconds, Maeve was impatient.

Maeve said, "Hey, you two, stop it. No secrets."

I tried my best to think of a plan. "Can we use the upward motion of the Morse code to mask us opening the bottom of the drop ship and fall out?"

"And fall onto what? Land? Ocean?"

Said Maeve, "I think we should open the door. This is hopeless. And besides, look at Taiga."

The ship had not stopped moving up and down in Morse code, though the message was repeating. Taiga looked green in the gills. She had vomited a little and then sheep-ishly covered it up with her paw in embarrassment. I went over and let her know it was OK with a small pat on the head.

Said Maddy, "OK, fine. They are going to split us up. Good luck, all."

§0.02.08

The metallic walls of the ship opened slightly into... another drop ship. A spherical one, like a Christmas ornaament, that shimmered green and surrounded us on all sides. But we couldn't escape through it—the outer sphere was filled with a thick gel that filled in everything between the walls of our drop ship and the walls of the outer one.

Maddy said, "Oh my gosh, of course. Brilliant." Somehow, the Adults had drop ship tech now.

A voice came from all sides, with a thick Indian accent. A deep, resonant, Adult voice. In his mid-forties, at least. "This is the first drop ship we've ever been able to make, Madeleine. The gel was my idea. I was hoping you'd be proud of us."

"Surya, so good to hear your voice," said Maddy, dryly.

"I must admit, it was fascinating watching you think up an entirely new physics to explain how we captured your ship. In fact, all we did was build a bigger one and filled it with a compression gel so that whenever your ship tried to move, we applied a current and the gel just canceled out the movement in the equal and opposite direction."

I got the sense that he was trying to impress Maddy. She would notice that too and use it. Somehow.

"Clever. Analog," said Maddy.

"And we have people unpacking your new physics models as we speak. Might even be a Nobel Prize in there for one of them. Does Sweden still exist? Well, if they do, I'm sure there's a Nobel somewhere in my future. Thinking of the ship as a particle? To whom do we owe that discovery?"

Maeve and Maddy looked at each other as women, knowingly.

Said Surya, "Adams. It makes sense to find you here, in a teardrop in the sky, doing nothing."

I laughed. "Madeleine tells me you disliked my pacifism," I said, louder perhaps than I should have. I didn't know where the speaker was in this strange metallic bubble.

Said Surya, "I believe that it was when the body count numbered above two billion that, yes, I started to blame you. At three billion, I got angry. At four, I decided that I would never, ever forgive you."

"I thought Madeleine was dead. I don't expect you to understand."

"One life? All because you grieved *one* life? You child."

"Surya, be nice," said Maddy.

It worked. Surya switched his attention to her.

"Madeleine, how'd you spoof the Colony Three thoughts?" asked Surya. "You really shouldn't have done that. We almost started World War IV trying to surround it."

"A simple dream."

"But real memories have a much higher sensory fidelity. We know the difference. There are all kinds of positional and bodily metadata when a memory is real. Did you really spoof all that?"

"I lucid dreamed it under control of my Bridge. Lucid dreams are more like perception than imagination. It wasn't hard. Remember, my pinky is doing more computational work than your entire fleet of soldiers and AIs, Surya," said Maddy. She was up to something. That bit about the pinky was an obvious lie, meant to elicit anger in anyone listening below Surya's rank. Of course, *he* wouldn't care. But his soldiers and his AIs, both listening, had their pride hurt.

Why did she want their pride hurt?

Taiga maintained a low growl at the continued sound of Surya's voice. Suddenly, the walls of the second drop ship opened and the gel changed shape, forming into a tunnel connecting the holes in the two drop ship walls.

We could walk through.

"Please, come in," said Surya. "Of course, don't try anything. We are in the middle of the ocean. Nobody can, what's the saying in your old movies? 'Nobody can hear you scream' out here."

Six soldiers appeared at the entrance, each outfitted in tactical armor with not a millimeter of skin showing anywhere, not even their eyes, which were covered by military-grade AR goggles. The Adults still needed the exoskeleton tech, like enhanced or AR vision. Children, though, just had their Bridges print proteins on demand to respond to different wavelengths of light or heat or anything in the electromagnetic spectrum and then shove those proteins into their retinas within seconds, as needed, a la carte. We didn't even have to think about it. If it was night out, we could see as well as a cat without even thinking about it—the infrared proteins were activated by darkness. If we needed to detect the Earth's magnetic field to navigate by dead reckoning. It just happened instinctively. It took a while sometimes to learn what the new sensory information meant, but the Bridge also did a decent job sculpting years of fake experience into the neurons in just a few minutes. I had almost forgotten how sense-poor the Adults were.

Maddy was plotting. The Maeve half of Maeve-Maddy had been silent, soaking it all in. Did the Adults know Maeve and Maddy were Crossed? I'm not sure they did. Behind the soldiers, an extremely thin man with glasses and a laptop looked past us and into the drop ship.

"Where's the dog?" asked the thin man. He was pressing buttons on his laptop, alternating between looking at its screen and into the ship. Taiga, tail wagging, ran to the thin man, stood between his legs, and growled.

Growled at me. At us.

"Good girl," said the thin man.

He must be controlling her Bridge somehow. Dogs had less prefrontal cortex than people to suppress some of the more pack-like, feral behaviors. I tried to situationally assess as much as I could. I stared at Taiga with pleading, familiar eyes, but it only enraged her further. Her teeth were bare, snarling. It was heartbreaking. The only time I had ever felt more defeated was when I learned— falsely, I know now—that Maddy had died.

The thin man said, "Split them up. Make sure Adams and Madeleine are never within speaking or touching distance. Put them in the Faraday rooms." He grabbed one of the soldiers, who appeared to be second in command, by the collar. "Listen to me." He spoke to the whole group of soldiers. "All of you. *Do. Not. Let. Them. Get. Close. To. Each. Other.* Do you understand? These are not normal people. These are the smartest people on Earth. They have some voodoo secret languages we can't even detect. At least, we think they do. We don't even know how they communicate. Whatever we think they are capable of; they are capable of more than that. You cannot even imagine their minds. It would be like an ant trying to imagine the plans of a human. Do you get it? Treat them like advanced AIs you don't understand. Not humans. You are the ants here. I am an ant, too, here. But I at least know what I don't know. They are learning a lifetime's worth of experience in their minds, every second, of every day. Their plan, when they make it, is going to be better than our best defense. You need to treat them like they are nuclear weapons. *Do. Not. Let. Them. Escape.*"

Which got me thinking: What *was* Maddy's plan? What would I do if I were her? The thin man went on, waving at Maddy: "This one has more computational power in her pinky than you and your entire family line going back to the Ice Age. Get it? Two soldiers per prisoner. Go." Odd.

The thin man repeated Maddy's line. He must have heard her say it, which means he was in the same room or on the same comms channel as Surya. Neurolinguistic programming? Or just a coincidence? Is that why she lied?

"Alpha, Delta, take this girl."

"Beta, Gamma, this one."

The two largest of the men were left over and they zip tied my hands. The soldier named Beta roughly grabbed Maddy's hand, twisting her elbow and arm. Maddy winced and fell to her knees. He had many patches on his sleeve. Coat of arms. Company patches from the War, which meant he was the sole survivor of entire companies of soldiers until he got sent to the next one. He had probably seen quite a lot. "In your pinky, huh?" he asked. He unfurled her hand and looked at her pinky finger. He then held it as if to break it. "So this is like unplugging a data center, then?" He broke it backwards. Maddy screamed. Maeve winced.

The two soldiers assigned to me grabbed my arms, lifting me slightly upwards as they carried me off, such that my toes were dragging on the ground, almost like I was *en pointe* in ballet. It reduced the number of surfaces I could push off to zero, just in case I had plans.

They were both tall, almost as tall as I was, each at least 6'8". Maybe professional athletes in another, more peaceful time. The three of us were also escorted by a few small drones in the shape of metallic spheres, each about the size of tennis balls. They made a small metallic hum, like a camera shutter going off thousands of times a second.

The terror crept above the amount my Bridge could suppress. For the first time since I could remember, I was just a bag of simple emotions. Fear. Survival.

Loss.

"What're these things?" I asked, nodding toward the floating spheres.

Silence.

"Are they cameras?" Silence.

"Little poison dart frogs, in case I escape?" Silence.

"You know, I—"

The last thing I remember of that corridor was one of the drones lighting up.

§0.02.09

I **woke up** in a cell. A white room. Maybe hours had passed. Maybe minutes. The only things in the room were a desk, a bed, and a toilet. And some soldiers. And Surya. And the thin man. Surya was directly in front of me. The thin man was behind him, with a laptop and a wire connected all the way to a needle in my arm.

I was wet, somehow. Surya threw another glass of water in my face.

"Wake up, Ali," said Surya.

It was a reference, I gathered, to Muhammad Ali, who sat out the Vietnam War.

"*Where is Madeleine?*" yelled the Admiral.

I had no idea what he meant.

"*How did she escape?*"

"I...what....did she? Maddy? Maeve?" I asked.

I was still groggy.

Surya paced in a tight circle, as if holding back the desire to punch me in the face. If this was a gambit on his part, he was bad at bluffing. This seemed real. The tight circle was a physical response to a real emotion he couldn't control. Besides, it broke every protocol of interrogation to have Surya, their Admiral, question me and reveal that Maddy had escaped. They should have tested to see if I was surprised Maddy was still on board to test what I knew. This was panic. Whatever Maddy's plan was, it worked.

157

"Eve?" I mumbled.

"Shut up. Where is Maddy?"

I looked down at the needle in my arm and traced the wire back to the thin man and his laptop. He looked at me, pressed a key, and stepped back. I think he expected me to react somehow.

I suddenly got really tired. Achingly, desperately so, and realized what had happened. The thin man had sent such severe pain signals through the needle that my Bridge, in order to suppress them, had expended about two days' worth of my metabolism. I didn't feel the pain, but the fatigue and the cost were real. I almost would have preferred the pain.

"His Bridge is good," said the thin man, who sounded impressed.

"Strongest I've ever seen. He didn't even wake up and I had the dial turned to ten. This is an eleven. And it's logarithmic."

"Where is Maddy?" repeated Surya. "Where is the Thirteenth? Where were you guys before we picked you up? That fake boat was a ruse."

"Taiga?"

"Yes, good, we didn't find any dog hair. So where were you? Tell me everything!"

The thin man stepped forward and put a light hand on Surya, a suggestion to calm down. Surya angrily brushed him off.

158

"He's not going to talk while he still has the Bridge, Admiral."

Still has? What did he mean, "still has"?

"Do it. He's useless," said Surya. "And once we get word to Madeleine that we removed his Bridge, she'll know we're serious. He'll be dead to her."

"What?" I asked. "You can't...what?"

I was groggy. This didn't make sense. Removing a Bridge was impossible. The Bridge and my brain had spent so much time growing together that they were practically the same thing. It was impossible to know what was Bridge and what was natural because a Bridge made *real* proteins. It used the same machinery that the cells themselves used as production centers. There was no difference at any level between natural and Bridge-made molecules.

The thin man's face wrinkled into a smile as he spoke to me: "I can only tell you this now because I know that in a few hours you will be too dumb to understand it. Every Bridge-made protein has a trace to it. It's a bit like how scientists can detect art forgeries from after nuclear testing in the early 20th century. Every single pigment of paint in the world became slightly radioactive. Bridges did something similar to all proteins. We don't know what, exactly, but we found a marker. We anesthetize you, fire up a fifty Tesla pulsed magnet with a bioprotective coating, look for the spin signature of Bridges, which recover slower for some reason, and obliterate them all in one zap. You'll keep some of the proteins and connections the Bridge already made, but it won't help you anymore. You'll be just as dumb as the rest of us. And according to our tests, actually, even dumber than the dumbest human. You rely on the Bridge like a curse. Your brain is mush without it. You are nothing without it. *You'll* be the ant, Adams. *You.*"

Unsure what to do, I looked behind him, at Taiga, for help. I tried thinking, *Come here, girl*, but in response, Taiga only bared her teeth at me.

§0.03.01

It was dark.

Not in the room.

In my mind.

But also in the room.

It was hard to notice the difference. But some part of me held onto a feeling that my memories of memories were brighter from Before. Now that it was After, my sight and sounds were as dim as the room I was stuck in.

Bed.

Desk.

Toilet.

Gray walls.

Paper.

Pen.

I'm going to keep writing things down in this memory palace just in case someone someday reads it. But I do worry. It doesn't come as easily as Before.

Please forgive me.

I keep being told by the nice guards that I was the smartest person on the planet. Ha. They say now that I'm dumber than an ant. I haven't seen an ant in years. Since I was small. I must concentrate.

Did I get surgery? My head doesn't hurt. I remember a line from a writer about how after he got shock therapy that they had cured the disease but lost the patient. Who was it? I can't remember. It is such a nice line that I wonder if maybe they did not kill all of the patient. Or did my sister say that? That's smart enough to be her idea.

"Bridge" is a strange word. I keep hearing the guards say it. Like the one in my hometown, that Maddy and I used to play under. She was always so much smarter than me. I fell off that bridge once. I found a bunch of old books on the bottom of the river after I splashed down and almost drowned. It was so cold. My eyes were open the whole time. Maddy had to dive in and save me. I wonder if that's what the guards mean.

Maybe if I start from the beginning. Try to think and write down everything I remember.

These are things I know are true: Maddy and I were born in Boston, at Mass General Hospital, on July 4, 2065. Maddy was first, a few minutes before me. The firstborn gets all the hormones because the blood cables get hooked up in serial, not in parallel. With twins, the next in line gets the washed-out hormones the first didn't need or use. That explains a lot. Or maybe it explains nothing.

I don't believe in that whole childhood trauma thing, even if childhood starts in the womb like some say. Our parents were both biological engineer professors at MIT on sabbatical to have us. Mom was a quantum geneticist and ran a lab trying to figure out the origins of life. Dad's job was as a molecular statistician, which mostly meant he was an idea concierge to the AI robot scientists who did all the theoretical work.

I didn't realize until much later that them taking the year off to have us meant we were experiments, not children.

They didn't need *time* to have us.

They needed *focus*.

Mom wanted us to be born in a stress-free boutique hospital, but Dad said that he only trusted hospitals that saw large numbers of similar problems. He trusted population averages. His theory was that doctors who see the most cases have the most experience and thus the best intuitions. He hated concierge doctors.

He might be right. Either way, Mom was *mad*. But Maddy and I came out healthy and normal. Dad was also hiding the biggest secret of all, even from Mom. We were IVF babies, of course, as all babies are these days. But what he didn't say was that he had been working with an old buddy of his from school and government, a doctor who also happened to be a doctor at Mass General, to give us a genetic advantage as babies beyond the normal stuff.

Dad's doctor friend injected Mom with some sort of device—I can't remember the name of it—during a routine checkup, but it went straight to our brains.

The same thing had been tried in a few Adults experimentally, but it never really caught on. Something about them being too old. Their neurons weren't rubbery enough.

Dad told Mom about it a few days after we were born. He explained that it was why he took the year off, to focus on Maddy and me. That we might be growing ten cognitive years in one with the device. That it was totally safe. And that Maddy and I were the next generation of humanity. (I know this because once Maddy and I started to understand spoken English a few months later, I was able to replay their verbal arguments like they were memories.)

Mom was *mad*. Oh my gosh. *So mad*. I don't think they knew we could hear or that we, at the time, were already able to speak to each other through a tactile language we developed while still inside Mom. I can't hear their arguments anymore for some reason, but I do vaguely re-member the emotional content.

Mom almost left Dad. It got bad. But he argued that this could be the very thing we needed to save the planet from ourselves. Really, I think it was just too much for Mom to imagine not sticking with us, so she stayed.

We were *her* kids, even if we were mules. Life happened so slowly, at first. Both Mom and Dad underestimated how much Maddy and I were seeing, growing, and learning. We started speaking at two months. We learned Typing in the third trimester, as our bodies floated near each other, so relative to that, learning grammar and syntax and verbs and all that was incredibly easy. By twelve months, we could read and write in every known language. Our favor-ites were the ancient languages. Speaking them was a bit harder—we needed to wait for our jaws and lips and throat to develop more.

But our eyes and ears were quite keen.

I think it helped having Maddy there. I would have been so alone without her.

She and I were able to talk and study and share what we had each learned every night. We filled in each other's blind spots. We combined our knowledge at the end of each day through Typing. That's how good a language it is.

Dad ended up taking an extra year from MIT to raise us after Mom went back to work, but I think the reason she went back was she never really was comfortable with our brains or how fast we grew. I could see it, sometimes. She would shudder when she thought we weren't looking. I think she thought we were monsters. I wish I had known then that if only we had been a bit less threatening, maybe Mom would have stayed.

Anyway, Dad started us on intense VR training around when Mom went back to work, as soon as he realized he wouldn't have to spend any more time on languages or basics like that.

It was fun, learning physics from Isaac Newton and Albert Einstein avatars, but the avatars were really just AIs smarter than either of them dressed as the famous scientists. Dad had to reprogram them to give us a faster rate of teaching and to undo the learning caps they usually placed on VR schools. We sailed through PhD-level math stuff after just a few months. He pulled a few government strings to get some programmers to open some threads on the US's national computing cloud just for us. He ended up spending a good chunk of his and Mom's savings on GPU cycles just so the AIs could challenge and teach us more and more and more.

I guess I was pretty smart, now that I think about it.

What happened? Did I hit my head? Did I fall off the bridge again?

Dad didn't tell anyone about our enhancements, of course. Ignoring the moral and ethical stuff, he even just technically didn't really know what to say about them. Besides, I don't think anyone would have believed him that it worked. Instead, we became his obsession.

School was horrible, of course.

Maddy and I had grown up mostly with each other and with the teaching AIs and Dad. No other children. (We didn't call them "Children" yet, because we didn't call adults "Adults" yet, until the War.) No other children would play with me. Maddy was better at it. She was a born leader. She had kids on the playground doing her bidding like they were domesticated pets of hers.

She rounded them up for her personal protection and would have them coordinate social games to her liking. It was intuitive to her, but never to me. I have no idea how. She just understood how to pull preschool social primate levers, I think.

We fought sometimes, too, like all siblings. I remember one day, in kindergarten, I got scared and tried to run up and hug her, to Type on her back, but she pushed me away and I tripped and fell into some mud. In front of everyone on the playground. I'll never forget that.

166

One day, Mom never came back. At all. Dad said she got a new job across the country and that we would see her eventually. For a while, new kinds of moms showed up to help Dad, every few months for years, but they were never as nice as Mom. They always had names from Ancient Greece, like Circe, Athena, Helen, and Cassandra. I'm not sure Dad noticed the pattern. We did.

They especially didn't like Maddy, not a single one of them.

Maddy told me her theory about the Greek names one day, that as babies stopped being made naturally, the last name became less and less important over time, so first names started taking more and more priority. And once Turkey took over Greece (this was before we were born) and tore down all the ancient ruins there, the Western countries decided to try to combat the rising Middle East by preserving history in a different way. So, Ancient Greek names became *very* popular for a while. It was a national effort to get in touch with our roots. This was all before the Great War, of course, when all the Adults banded together.

I had to stay home from school for a year while Maddy, Ms. Popular, went without me. When she came home, she would go straight to her room. It hurt. Even worse, Dad had remarried, to a woman named Ariadne, who *really* didn't like me.

She would yell. A lot. I was always in trouble at home. I got used to being punished by her. I think the enhancement would kick in and reduce my pain sensitivities. Once her hand stopped working as punishment, she started using a wooden spoon if I got in trouble, which seemed to be almost every day. I knew what was about to happen anytime I saw her with it.

It was always something I did. I didn't put things away properly. I used words she didn't understand. I played for too long in the backyard. I think Ariadne really resented having to care for me. She ignored Maddy, but with me, she showed no mercy. I was growing very fast—already taller than most girls even my age—but she often sent me to bed hungry. Called me a pig for asking for seconds. Really, I don't know why. Dad had explained the enhancement to Ariadne and she didn't take it well. One day, she threatened me. Said she had been to a doctor and he knew how to reverse the enhancement and that if I didn't behave, she was going to send me to the doctor and get it removed. I had never been so scared.

I remember that night so well. It was when I got sick for the first time. I was maybe around age five or so. It felt like I had lost my brain. I couldn't do much. I even forgot how to Type. I had a bad fever for a very long time. It felt sort of like right now. That something was missing. That I was missing something. That a piece of me was gone.

Dad didn't really fight much for me. He lost interest in raising us once Mom left and he seemed to trust Ariadne, I think because of how much older she was than Dad. Almost ten years older. She was very good at caring for him but not for us. She acted like she was from a different time.

From the 1950s. Ariadne's son from her first marriage didn't seem to have done much with himself. I wonder if that was the reason she hated me. He had flunked out of high school and joined the military and died in the first of the wars over Greece in a friendly fire accident. I only met him once before that. He seemed very distant.

Maddy asked if I was OK a few times after she saw Ariadne punishing me, but I think secretly she liked being the golden child.

It wasn't all bad. The good times were lovely, when Maddy and Dad were home. I read a lot when I wasn't in school and Maddy was. Ariadne would hide books from me, especially the ones I liked the most, to try to get me to go outside more.

She only left me with the ancient language books, probably because she didn't understand them and thought they were religious and that maybe a little religion would be good for me. My favorites by far were stories about the battles between the gods believed in by the ancient humans. Oh, and the Gnostic texts, which were always a challenge to translate from the Coptic, but I enjoyed it. The stories were so wild. So different. The origin of *everything*. They felt like they came from a time so long ago as to be almost a different planet entirely.

Ariadne used to yell at me and tell me I would never be Indiana Jones. She was right, I suppose.

§0.03.02

It's **been weeks now** in this room.

They haven't given me anything to do.

I'm so bored.

Someone named Admiral Surya and a very thin man who always has a laptop have stopped by twice to check on me, but they asked me the strangest questions. About a girl named Maeve, whom they insist I know. And if I have any idea why she is so sick. And about where Maddy is. But truly I have no idea. I can't remember much from the last few years. Mostly just my childhood.

Everything else is fuzzy.

The food is good. I sleep well.

I'm pretty happy. Life is simple in here.

But I keep having the same nightmare every night. I fall off the bridge. The whole dream is in black and white. The water is clear, and at the bottom of the river are old, moldy books and shards of paper. I've started to be able to read the titles and text, but it takes a lot of effort. I'm hoping one night I'll be able to open one of the books in the dream.

I don't know which to grab, but they are all so close. Every time I try, right as I'm about to touch the text, I hear Maddy splash into the water and she grabs me and pulls me out. As soon as our heads clear the water, everything is in color again. And then she yells at me, but I can't tell what she's saying.

My hand keeps moving toward the Gnostic book with the best stories, especially the redo of Plato. I remember that one well. For a while, it was my absolute favorite. I used to have it under my sheets. I remember it so well because I was reading it when I first became sick and it was the book I was holding when I suddenly became well again. I love that book.

The thin man has visited me a few more times but he doesn't say much.

It feels like he is playing mind games with me, like a cat with a mouse. He has a laptop he always looks down at while he's talking to me. Always asks about Maeve. She is getting sicker and sicker, apparently. They don't know why. They said she's an addict and that she's in withdrawal. But they can't find any drugs in her system or even traces of the lack of them.

They ask me if I saw her take any drugs when I knew her, but I swear I don't even know her. I tell that to the thin man but he never believes me.

He also said that things are changing soon. Apparently, things got really bad between the Children and Adults at Colony Three. A war almost broke out.

And they agreed to give me over to the Children in negotiations.

How exciting!

I can get out of here finally.

He laughed when he said it, so I know good things must be coming. I'm going to be with my people. Kids my age.

Outside. Fresh air. He said someone named Washington is going to take care of me from now on and that they are going to hand me over tomorrow. He said that with a smile. I don't know why I'm so important but if it gets me out of here, I don't care.

Personally, I can't wait.

This Washington must be an old friend of mine.

I sure do owe him one.

§0.03.03

The spaceship I got to ride on was so fun.

It was like being inside a soap bubble made of metal from the future. And the flight was only a few minutes. It was like teleporting. I tried touching the metal walls and a friendly kid in a uniform told me not to and that I might get my hand stuck in there forever.

I like my new room even better.

The Children are much nicer to me than the Adults ever were. Washington especially, who as soon as I arrived gave a speech to the entire Colony with me right here on stage next to him. He made me give a speech too, which was surprising and awkward. I didn't say much. Just sort of babbled. I could see the Children were disappointed in how little I said but Washington seemed quite content with it.

All the Children applauded when it was mentioned that I would get what I deserved, which I presume is the right to be home again and maybe see Maddy. They mentioned a dog and said she was here too. And I think I heard this right, that she had crossed paths with a pack of other dogs they brought to the island and that animals were allowed again. The crowd of Children cheered at that.

They said they had to restrain me for my own safety. I trust them. I think it is because I'm so much taller than everyone.

My new room is much bigger than my old room. It has a desk and a few books and I get paper and pens and a wall screen to watch television on. I could stay here forever.

Everybody wants to know where Maddy is. I tell them all I can: that I don't know.

Every day, they make me see a girl. I think she's about ten years old, give or take. (I'm not allowed to ask her about her). She has been asking me about my dreams. She keeps asking about Maddy. Why is she there in the dream? What does she look like? What does she want? Did the dream really happen? What age is Maddy? Questions like that. Most importantly, she is trying to get me to figure out what Maddy says to me right after rescuing me from the water.

It's actually a fun puzzle. I look forward to sleeping and having the dream so I can talk about it more with the girl. She comes to my room every morning. I wish she would tell me her name. I started calling it my "bridge dream," which always gets a funny look from her.

She also keeps asking also about what they did to me to turn me into an ant, which is her nickname for me. Good morning, Ant. See you tomorrow, Ant. What are you reading, Ant?

One day I explained that the clearest book at the bottom of the water in the dream is a copy of the Gnostic texts and that I grew up with the book. I explained a few details I remembered about it. That the book was large, like a photography book, and had footnotes along the margins of each page. I asked if she could maybe get me a copy. Maybe something inside would help me remember?

She said that was a good idea and thanked me for my cooperation. It was a strange thing she had said. Why *wouldn't* I cooperate? She went outside for a moment and when she returned said she had asked a linguist from Colony Nine and that a copy of the book should be here shortly by drop ship.

She asked what the book was and why I liked it. I told her I read it at night to try to wish Ariadne away. She asked who Ariadne was and I said I didn't really want to talk about it. I said, "My stepmom," and the girl seemed to get it. She had sympathy for me. The world was like a dark German fairy tale now. All Adults were bad in the eyes of all Children.

A few minutes later the book arrived and she handed it to me. I was thrilled.

This was it!

I held it by the spine and shook it, with the pages downward. I always used to do that to find the page I was last on in my copy. The physicality of a book's spine had a kind of memory to it, just like we do.

I flipped through it until one page made me pause. It was the cover of the book from my dream! I told the girl I recognized this page. That it was from the bridge dream. I read it out loud and—

§0.03.04

I wish I could explain what happened to me. Some things are beyond words. It was like snapping awake while already being awake. I realized exactly where and who I was. Everything just popped into my awareness again.

And I mean *everything.* The facts were clear as day. I was Bridged. Again. I was Adams. Again. We were on New Zemlya. Of course we were.

Also, strangely, I was Crossed with Taiga. Her body both froze and growled in the first moments of the Crossing, but her tail also wagged as she growled—I think, mostly, out of confusion. I was confused too. If I had a tail, I don't know what it would do. (I suppose I *do* have a tail now but no way to control it?) I tried the equivalent of patting Taiga on the head through the Crossing by activating the sensory-motor pathways that would otherwise be activated by the real thing. It seemed to work. It took a few seconds, but I quickly figured out an asymmetry in the Crossing between our respective minds' metabolisms and information-processing capacities, which I then used to suppress the Crossing for the time being. I was still Crossed with her, technically, but we could be separate for a little while. I would have to investigate it more later, but I think the trick exploited the fact that we were different species and different minds.

It was glorious being right of mind again. Being back. It was as if the world was once again in cognitive Technicolor. I was back in Oz. The world outside me didn't just exist anymore. Its details were clues. The whole cognitive apparatus of imagination and memory, two sides of the same coin, snapped back into place. Even the smudges and cracks on the walls and door and each of the objects in the room suddenly became clues. And I replayed and analyzed every gesture and word of the girl, my interrogator. I concluded that though she appeared like a soldier, she was dressed down to appear casual, which I hadn't realized before.

I could now even see the tiny video camera in the corner of her eye, near or inserted into the tear duct, which was how Children's special ops teams shared information. I was being watched. By everyone. All the time. Of course I was.

My interrogator could tell something was different in me, but I don't think she knew what. I don't think she could have possibly dreamt up the reality of what had happened or why. And whoever was watching, no matter their vigilance, their guard would probably be down after weeks of this because their first assumption will always be that I'm still Bridgeless and therefore no longer dangerous. Whereas before, they were trained to remain defensive when they didn't understand my intention. Watching my fall from intellectual grace was probably rewarding for them, which would hopefully keep them from noticing any change.

I would need to act slowly to keep up the charade that my Bridge was still gone.

My interrogator would likely misinterpret all of the little details about my behavior until she had overwhelming reason to believe otherwise. She would give all kinds of other causes to my change in demeanor because she needed to take credit for it. She was biased to need to see changes that were her doing. That was a weakness.

Every few seconds my Bridge was reactivated, I realized more and more. This was a crucial window where I had to keep playing dumb.

I reasoned through a few conclusions based on what I had observed these past few months. One, Washington didn't need me alive. *He needed Maddy alive.* His Bridge probably still prevents him from thinking about her without severe pain. Which means that the girl in the room, if she's Bridged, must be in constant pain given that she asks me about Maddy every day. Maybe that meant...of course...there was only one conclusion. She's not a soldier. She's a fellow prisoner. The tear duct camera is involuntary and my interrogation is her ticket out of here. If she gets me to reveal Maddy's location, then she gets set free. That was another weakness. I can use that.

"What's your room like?" I asked.

She stared at me and remained silent. This was the first time I had really asked about her existence beyond the room we were in. Did that indicate a new cognitive capacity to think beyond the present? Perhaps. I should be more careful, but the gamble was worth it as the real reason I was here dawned on me. Washington must have brought me back to Colony Six to parade me in front of the rest of the Children to weaken their hope that there was any alternative to him as leader. I had, after all, been one of the hallowed few; the prodigal son, returned at long last after the War. Washington had seen the admiration in other Children's eyes as they looked at or spoke to or about me, an admiration that must have bothered him.

He knew his standing was shaky. Probably, some other Children close to him suspected or knew he was the real Convention bomber. Not Maeve nor I, as the media said. At the very least, I'm sure rumors got around and he wouldn't be the first authoritarian to stage a bombing to get grip on the reins. Sacrificing me was a good strategy to ruin dissident hope. If anyone had put any faith at all in me previously, it would be undone seeing me Bridgeless, hope-less, and simple.

In other words, I was propaganda. My simplicity was a tool.

Some things I still hadn't worked through. Had the Adults *really* removed my Bridge? How? The ability to remove a Bridge is an existential, world-changing tech-nology on par with its creation. It would completely destabilize the world order if Children could voluntarily or by force remove Bridges. On the most basic level, it meant that Children could be punished in a way never possible before. The details of my Bridge removal are murky, as if it happened before a long, complicated surgery. Probably what the thin man had said about the high-T magnet was true. (In theory, the physics held.) Which meant, I suppose, that I was propaganda for the Adults, too. If I could be rendered Bridgeless and simple, then so could anyone. If Bridges were removed out of all or even some Children, humanity would spin back into a Dark Age.

I was sent back as a bartering chip, but also as a warning: If it could happen to Adams, it could happen to you.

I was back but aware enough to realize I was not entirely back. I couldn't for the life of me recall how I got my Bridge back. Was it the same one? Had the book reactivated it? Some phrase I said aloud? Was it just meant to happen after a certain time? Had I built a fail safe? I had no idea. I couldn't recall. I could tell I knew the answer, but it must be taxing for me, and it would take at least a few nights of sleep for the Bridge to fully integrate through the rest of my brain and be exactly as before. Which meant that I should hang out here for a few days if possible. It would be dangerous to escape before I was ready.

In the meantime, I could try to figure out what was going on. Where was everyone? I had no idea where Maddy was. Taiga was outside, still wagging her tail, knowing that she knows I'm alive and near. Maeve must still be with the Adults, which explains why she's in severe withdrawal. *She's still Crossed to Maddy.* I winced in shared pain. Every moment of her existence must be excruciatingly painful right now. Maddy is probably halfway around the world and encrypting all her thoughts and fleeing, all while Maeve is in jail going through some serious psychic withdrawal—way worse than any addictive drug's absence.

I needed to bide my time until fully recovered, but after that the steps were clear. I needed to get out of the room. I needed to rescue Maeve. And then I needed to find Maddy, wherever she was in the world.

I figured my only way out was if I gave my interrogator enough information about Maddy so she believed she'd succeeded in her job enough to convince Washington he didn't need me anymore. Likely, he'd then stage a public execution. I'm the bomber, after all, according to his twisted view of history. And he'll make everyone watch, just like in the old days.

That's my way out.

"So, I think I get it now," I said.

"Oh?" said the girl.

"Yes. The book, thank you. I can hear now what Maddy is saying. I translated it. She's saying, 'Meet me on the oil rig.'"

Her pupils dilated. She sat straighter and wrote something down.

"And what exactly does that mean, do you think?"

"I don't know."

"Come on, Adams, help me out here."

"Help you out?"

"I mean, come on," said the girl. "What *might* 'oil rig' mean?"

"What's your name?"

"I've told you a hundred times. It's Wren."

"Really, I don't remember that. I'm sorry. Hi, Wren."

"Focus, Adams."

"Maddy used to say she loved being where the magnets are the weakest. That's all I remember. Somewhere in the largest waters. With the boat we were on?"

Largest...waters? *You mean "oceans"?* Pretending to be simple was a skill unto itself, harder than I thought. And maybe even a tad foolish since I needed to lay low for a few days until I was at full strength. Just like in any board game, where it is easy to tell if one's opponent is losing on purpose because their moves are detectably below their usual ability, my being too simple would be as big a giveaway as my being too smart. I got lucky this time. My information reveal about the oil rig was too exciting. And the idea that I had suddenly reacquired my Bridge from inside my jail cell was unlikely to be on anybody's radar. The oil rig story masked my feint, but it might not have tricked others watching. I should be careful for a few days. Say very little. Only what was essential. I needed to toe a fine line between simple and non-aberrant.

Wren was visibly excited; almost trembling. She looked like a prisoner released from chains. Before she stood and left the room, she looked me in the eye.

"Thank you," she said.

I could see her seeing me. Something about her eyes made it seem like she could tell. Could tell I was faking it.

But maybe she didn't care. She needed out, too and it had been a plausible enough story and new enough data to them to sound real. If they checked it against the Adults' story about them finding a fake boat, all the details would check out too. They would know about the oil rig but think it was at the bottom of the ocean. It was a Hail Mary gamble. I was putting Maddy in serious danger if my plan didn't work and she was back there somehow. But the only path forward was if they thought that Maddy was trying to send me one last message and for them to think *they* decoded the message.

The shortest path to mind control is tricking people into thinking it was their idea in the first place.

Hopefully by now Maddy had expected and anticipated the worst—that, without a Bridge, I would reveal the oil rig location under duress. I was proud that I hadn't; at least, not without wanting to.

When Wren returned, she was extremely serious. She wouldn't look me in the eye as she stood aside the open door, staring at the wall. I soon learned why.

Washington himself entered the room.

"Adams, old boy," said Washington. He wasn't even flanked by security. It was just the three of us in the room. He must not even remotely suspect me. I said nothing.

"Our team is headed to the oil rig as we speak," said Washington. "Thank you, Wren, for getting the confession out of him. He always had a soft spot for tall girls from Colony Six. Or maybe it's just Maeve."

"Adams, meet Wren." He gestured toward Wren, who seemed to have slunk in the corner. "Do you recognize her? Tell me you do, Adams. It is Maeve's sister, of course. I figured it might stir up some…familiar feelings."

I stood up. But without glancing at me and while still looking away, Wren shook her head slightly. She was telling me to back down.

Washington went on: "We'll find the rig and maybe even Maddy before it settles at the bottom of the ocean, don't worry. And if not, we'll just treat it like a derelict ocean liner. It will be a coral reef. Maybe even a boutique diving excursion for all the submarine and dive hobbyists out there, one day." I said nothing.

"Though," said Washington, as he snapped his fingers and excitedly pointed towards me, "to be honest, you might not like what's next, I'm afraid, Adams. We had a military trial. You had a lawyer who did their best but unfortunately, in light of the overwhelming evidence, you've been sentenced to a public hanging. It's barbaric, really. Straight nineteenth-century stuff. I'm embarrassed, actually. But my hands are tied."

I sat back down. Buried my head in my hands. Pretending to mourn my own fate, simply.

"Wren, you are free to go. Adams, stay a bit longer, won't you? Tomorrow, at sunrise, you die."

§0.03.05

Only once I was roughly pulled out of sleep the next morning did I realize that I hadn't slept well in months. Without the Bridge controlling my brain's oscillations, my simpler brain had been at the unpracticed whim of natural sleep and had been terrible at it. But through the night, with my Bridge returned, it went into overdrive and simulated all the trillions of possible pasts and futures as it got to work repairing itself and me.

With a hood over my head, I was escorted to a large, open courtyard. Just as I suspected, I was in New Zemlya again. I heard the clamor of thousands of Children below and the spaciousness of the outdoor cavern we were in. The whole Colony had been forced to stop what they were doing for a few early morning minutes to watch.

As I was brought on stage, with the hangman's hood still over my head, I heard the crowds before me—a sea of Children, a few whose voices I recognized from the Convention. I suddenly recalled all the gaps in a series of flashes. My childhood. Ariadne. Maddy. The sickness that wasn't.

Of course.

That's how I got the Bridge back.

I had a backup.

Washington was next to me, at the pulpit, speaking to the gathered crowd. "Citizens of New Zemlya, it is with great sadness we gather today," he said. The audience turned silent. Mournful. "A military tribunal has found Adams, whom we once held in high esteem, who we once treated as a hero, guilty of sedition, treason, and murder. The sentence is death." I could hear him turn to me. He put a friendly hand on my shoulder. "We still don't know why, Adams. Why? Why did you do this? What did you hope to accomplish by murdering your fellow man?"

The details, as they flooded back about my childhood, shocked me. I must have been quite the clever child. I had programmed my own Bridge recovery process in the event I ever lost it, but I hadn't at the time suspected Adults or Children or anything like that. There had been no War yet. Nobody even knew I was Bridged at the time, except my immediate family, Ariadne, and maybe a few others my dad had told along the way.

The whole thing was not a preparation for this War-slung world I lived in now. I hadn't anticipated anything. *I had, in fact, been terrified of Ariadne.* I was so scared of her taking away my Bridge when she had threatened to that I had made a copy of its workings, and a kind of compiler to bring it back. I stored the workings deep in the epigenetic structures of my cells. There was no way to remove this copy without killing me.

It was stored in my cellular machinery as topological information on the surface of newly made proteins in the brief window in which they folded into their final shape. The information was not in the Bridge-made proteins themselves, which the Adults had been able to detect—and somehow, with their magnets, remove—but as intermediate steps in the conformational shaping of a protein. It was entirely undetectable and would always be because each shape lasted only a few, unsuspecting nanoseconds. But in those few nanoseconds I had stored the instructions on how to make a new Bridge, as if it was a biological compiler built atop the ribosome, nature's original compiler. I got the idea from one of the chemistry textbooks Mom wrote. I had told nobody, not even Maddy.

Heck, *I* didn't even really know. Only my subconscious did. I hid it from myself. That was necessary. And I hadn't been as sickly a child as I appeared to be. The whole time I was solving protein folding and backing up my Bridge just in case Ariadne's threat with the doctor to remove my Bridge was real. It was a monumental effort for my Bridge and I to encode a backup, which wore down my body. The hardest part was coming up with a foolproof plan to execute the backup once my Bridge was removed, which required me to simulate what it would be like to be without a Bridge.

The solution I came up with was similar to a dead-man's switch. Every morning I gave myself an elliptical cryptography test involving a riddle that my cerebellum had to unconsciously solve. If I didn't solve it after three consecutive days, the problem got a little easier (solvable, perhaps, by an Einstein- or Gödel-level intelligence in a lifetime of work). This was there as a kind of warning buffer just in case I hit my head or had a virus or fever or normal illness that reduced my cognitive capacity. If I didn't solve *that* problem for three days, the problem got even easier, to a graduate-level computational topology problem. Alan Turing stuff. Quantum holography. Basic stuff. And if still, after nine days of failure, I had solved nothing, then my brain would conclude it had a problem— that it was Bridgeless, why else couldn't I solve the riddle?—and it would trigger the dream.

I had coded the dream to be the same every night. It had to be simple, with basic symbolism, about bridges and books, so that my Bridge-less mind would understand. It was packed with clues and would repeat every night until I uttered a specific line from one of the Gnostic texts from the underwater book in the dream. I would have gotten to it eventually, slowly, maybe in a few more months, on my own. The text was arbitrary, just the equivalent of a long cryptographic cipher. Those books were my favorite as a kid so I must have picked the phrase from them. Wren had unwittingly, through what she thought was strategic kindness, brought me the key to my escape.

I had said nothing to the crowd for a few seconds. In fact, I had been busy reactivating my Crossing with Taiga. From her vantage, now our vantage, I learned that Taiga was indeed Crossed with every other dog in the Colony. Through the brief flits of our collective consciousness, I saw myself from various angles in a flashbulb of binocular rivalries, like flipping through a scrapbook. It was one of the early, confusing stages of Crossings. It didn't just happen.

Whatever the collective creature was that contained myself, Taiga, and her pack, we were essentially born into the world anew, at this very moment, and our brains had to learn to make sense of what they was taking in. It took training to see the world as a single, unified thing through multiple points of view. But Taiga, the pack, and I didn't have time to go through all the intense training the Zero Ball teams did to become a cohesive whole. No, we had to act. Now.

I could see a semblance of myself on stage and the thronged, huge pack of Children between Taiga and me. There were twelve other dogs plus Taiga, so I had my Bridge quickly write a program to coordinate their control as if they were each appendages and I was the body controlling them. As the twelve sprinted between the legs of the Children and through the crowd toward the stage, I felt like a conductor controlling the most complicated symphony imaginable. Twelve full, entire mammalian consciousnesses were subroutines to my brain and as I stood perfectly still on stage, nobody could quite imagine the extraordinary cognitive stress I was under just to maintain control of each. I was Bach. I was Stravinsky. Not that they had time to notice. All eyes had turned to the pack, which was sprinting toward the stage for reasons nobody, except me, understood.

Remarkably, because I was Crossed with the whole pack, each who knew the scent of every Child in the colony individually, it meant that identifying people out of the crowd was a lot easier than it would be by human sight alone. I immediately knew the identities of all of Washington's security detail—there were only three trained special ops soldiers surrounding him, guarding him—and so I had each of the dogs head toward and attack only those Children.

It worked. For a few seconds, each of the security members was distracted enough that their attention broke off toward the well-being of their siblings—just enough to let Taiga sneak through and, in one smooth leap, remove the hood from my head.

"Heel," I shouted. Boomed. Through the whole cavern. It was unfair to say, but no other Child had been through full puberty on this Colony. I sounded, to everyone's alarm, like an Adult. I needed to speak to them in a way no other Child could.

Through the Crossing, I had made the dogs stop their attacks simultaneously but I wanted to make it seem like, instead, they listened to me for some reason. The mystical explanation may yet still be a more powerful, or at least confusing, and therefore cognitively taxing, explanation than the real reason. Taiga stood at my feet, between myself and Washington, growling.

The whole room froze. I was still in chains, but the events had paralyzed everyone. Even Washington and his guards saw in Taiga the unmistakable intent that, were anyone at all to move, she would lunge for Washington's throat and rip it out.

"I need no preamble. What I need is your trust," I yelled, to the entire Colony. I didn't need a microphone like Washington did. The whole room could hear my booming, operatic voice.

"I would like to submit to a Fidelio Test. I did not bomb the Convention. Washington did. And I have proof. Scan my brain and find the recording."

Washington was close enough to the podium that the microphone picked up his response, broadcasting it. At first, his voice cracked.

"Oh, dear Adams, you think a few dogs and a claim of innocence from a dying man will change these people's minds? You are too simple to undergo a Fidelio. You don't even have a Bridge. We can't access the raw sensory stream recording."

"You can. I am Bridged. I have been this whole time. The Adults tricked you."

I lied. Simply, so that right now I didn't have to explain how I got my Bridge back from inside a jail cell.

"Impossible," said Washington.

"Tell your guards to stand down. I will undergo a Fidelio Test right here," I said. "Right now. You will all know exactly what happened on that day from my point of view. I can tell you all the exact words I heard, from Washington's

191

mouth: 'Plan Omega. Third option. Lock the doors. Blow them up.' What is Plan Omega, Washington?"

Washington paled. I don't know how, but the twelve dogs in the crowd had all been tranquilized. It was just Taiga and me now.

"Kill him," said Washington, to his guards. "I don't care if this dog bites me a little. We can fix that."

The guards hesitated.

And then, the crowd started to boo.

"All I ask is a Fidelio," I said. "I have undergone the upgrade as well. I can Cross. You can all see and know what happened that day. If I am guilty, it will show you that. And it will show you my reasons, as well. Isn't that what you just asked for, Washington? You can then have peace knowing you executed the right man. But if I am innocent, don't you all want to know? Don't you all want to see who your leader, this man, really is?"

It was my last gambit. Washington spoke half to me, half to the crowd: "How do we know the Adults didn't implant false memories? The Fidelio will show nothing reliable."

"You know as well as I, as well as everyone in this room, that is impossible."

A Fidelio Test was as close to lie detection as the world had. It didn't exactly tell you whether a person was lying or telling the truth at any given moment, but it did give something like an objective account of things. Relative to the massive amounts of storage and computation of a human brain, the external sensory stream into a human brain was actually quite a miniscule number of bits. And synthetic DNA storage allowed storage of information in a huge array of molecular letters, not just A T G C. Bridges could easily keep a raw archive of all external sensory data experienced by a person going back to the day the Bridge was installed. This was also one of the key parts to a Bridge's workings since it could constantly rehearse and replay older memories to learn from. But one quirk of synthetic DNA is that there was literally no way to alter the data. A single alteration rendered the entire archive void; it was a one-way zipper.

But the raw sensory data was useless on its own. It needed a human brain to interpret the data stream, so the Fidelio Test also required that the suspect Cross with a secure, organoid-AI hybrid brain whose only job was projecting the raw stream. And because I could Cross, thanks to Maddy's injection, I could undergo a Fidelio Test.

"How convenient," said Washington. "You show up Bridged and Crossed at just the right time to project false memories to us. If you are Bridged, like you say, how do we know you do not have an ability we don't understand to forge the sensory archive?" He turned to the crowd, but he could see they were not entirely on his side anymore. Doubt was in the air. Too many rumors had persisted, perhaps, for too long. "Is not rule number one about interpreting Adams and Madeleine—" Here, Washington, and much of the crowd, winced in pain at the thought of

193

Maddy. Her hack was still active. "Ah, sorry everyone. Is it not rule number one that we must assume that Adams can do things we cannot? That he was Bridged long before us? Have we forgotten this basic rule so quickly?"

A voice cried from the crowd: "Let him test!"

More chimed in. "Fidelio! Fidelio! Fidelio!"

Washington had no choice. He had to let me take the test. His people would never trust him if he didn't. Not with my accusation hanging in the air like acid rain.

"Fine, fine, fine," said Washington. "Bring out the Ma'at organoid and conduct the test. We will hang Adams after the fact. After we all see, firsthand, his treachery."

This surprised me. How could he possibly acquiesce so easily? We both knew that the Fidelio Test would show his guilt. What was his plan? It all happened quickly after that. It didn't take long for his plan to reveal itself. During the commotion and excitement, as the crowd realized it was going to see a Fidelio projection, and Ma'at had started projecting my brain's raw, interpreted version of the bombing, Washington ran. The crowd, enraptured by the Fidelio projection, started booing and hissing until, at last, when the echo of Washington's memory finally said the fateful words, the go signal for the bombing, they all turned to see their leader fleeing through the back of the tunnel, the very first tunnel I had walked through when I first saw the colony, where it had all seemed so calm so long ago, when I had woken up that morning in Norway, with Taiga and not a worry in the world. Simpler days.

The drop ships were on the other side of the tunnel and when Washington and his team approached a drop ship, the metallic wall opened for him. He looked back one last time at his people, whom he knew he could never return to. At this point, he knew his only option was to defect to the Adults and hope for life as a traitor. He ordered the three loyalist guards to stay behind and defend, to make sure nobody could trace or spot where he was headed. What he hadn't expected was how quickly the head of the military intelligence cabinet, in charge of information security for the Colony, on seeing the Fidelio projection, would revoke Washington's security clearance and, therefore, his access to walk through walls.

As he stood in the doorway to the drop ship and prepared one last triumphant gesture, the metallic walls, which no longer recognized his passage, closed on his body, severing it from its life.

The entire colony had witnessed Washington's death. Their Bridges, in unison, grieved and mourned the shock in mere seconds. As they turned toward me, with Taiga by my side, the Children seemed relieved.

Without provocation or conversation, I knew my role. I was to lead, for now.

"Do not celebrate," I said to the entire colony. I had my Bridge dehydrate my larynx and dilate the capillaries near my lungs to give them their fullest, silverback capacity. I needed these next words to be carved into each of these Children's souls as if by arrowhead.

"I need the best Zero Ball team we have. Who steps forward?"

It seemed obvious that everyone knew who that meant. The best of the very best. Their names were known.

Three girls and two boys stepped forward. "Are you the best Zero Ball team in the world?" They nodded, in unison. "Come with me. Everyone else, let me be very clear. I will lead. For now. Until I set a few things right. And then I will pass the torch to only that leader who seeks peace with the Adults. Your job, while I am gone, is to figure out who that is. Give it your all. And please, everybody, do me a favor. Do not report this news to the world for another thirty minutes exactly. Exactly. To the second. Starting right.... *now*. Pretend what you saw here didn't happen. Raise your hand if I have your word. Your silence. Your bond."

Every single Child, to the last, raised his hand.

§0.03.06

Time was of the essence. We were going to rescue Maeve. I pulled the commander of military intelligence, the same person who had rescinded Washington's access clearance, into the war room. I needed someone unafraid to take immediate and permanent action.

"Name?"

"General Jay, sir."

"Good work earlier. I will commend you later. Who has the most experience with naval battles from the War?" I asked.

"Admiral Maher, sir."

"Bring him here. Also, did we have any POWs who were ever aboard an Adult carrier?"

"Yes, sir, two special ops soldiers. They were unharmed."

"Bring them here, too," I said.

My voice was deeper than it had ever been. General Jay left briefly to bark orders to a subordinate, leaving only myself, the Zero Ball team, and a full wall of surveillance screens. I turned to the team.

"Do you have a team name?" The tallest girl took a step forward.

"We do, sir. Team 5150," she said.

"Nobody outside questioned that you were the best team. Why is that?"

"Well, sir," said the same girl, "we've won the World Cup this year as well as...well, every game we've ever played."

"You're undefeated? Even when you were first learning?"

"Yes, sir. We are all siblings. Fraternal quintuplets, actually. We really didn't need to do much training. We've been coordinated since we were born, in a way."

"I'm going to ask you to help me on an extremely dangerous rescue operation. I am loath to commit five members of the same family to the one operation, however. That violates an unspoken rule of war in the twentieth century, so that entire families don't get wiped out at once. Forgive my blunt talk, but time is of the absolute essence. I need your uncoerced consent and for you to volunteer before we proceed."

"You have it," said the girl.

"You don't need to think about it? Talk it over?"

"We just did," she said.

"All of you?"

They nodded in unison.

"Alright, thank you. Here's the plan. In twenty minutes and thirteen seconds exactly, news will spread around the world of Washington's death and my assumption of leadership of the Colonies and of all the Children. The Adults are going to panic but I am immediately going to head into the lion's den, to the carrier, and I am going to offer the world a salve. I am going to offer peace. They will be half an hour behind in their assumptions and not realize that we actually had time to plan a rescue operation."

"Sir, you said earlier the Adults did not remove your Bridge. So, are you working with them?" asked one girl.

"Good question. They did. That is a danger if you are captured. Please know that. I had a backup Bridge," I said, with a smirk. "But you may not. When you return, as heroes, I will explain it all to you."

Just then, General Jay, Admiral Maher, and two Children who couldn't be a lick over age seven entered the room.

"Introductions later, when we celebrate," I said to the room. All were rapt.

"Admiral Maher, in nineteen minutes exactly the world will receive news that Washington is dead," I said. "Two minutes later, I will get in a drop ship and fly to the UNS Hunley. Do not look confused, Admiral. Confusion is a waste of time. Between now and then, with proper speed, I need you and General Jay, with help from these two, who have been on the ship and been in its prisoner's quarters, to come up with a hostage extraction plan. Assume the hostage is incapacitated. The only personnel to attempt the extraction will be the members of Team 5150 here. I do not know where the prisoner is being kept. Her name is Maeve. Here is her picture."

"Sir, of course I know and admire 5150. They are sporting legends." He turned to the siblings. "And no offense to you personally but they are not military trained.

We have special ops teams for this that have trained their whole lives."

"So do the Adults, Admiral. That's exactly who they would plan for."

"Sir, I—"

"The matter is closed, Admiral. Thank you for trusting me. You all may have this room. I don't need it. I want to know as little about the plan as possible if I am unceremoniously captured and my Bridge removed, yet again, I do not want to know the details. And let me be very clear here. Your mission, should I also be captured, is to rescue Maeve. Not me. You may attempt to rescue me at some other time in the future. But really, I don't mind either way. But you must. I repeat, *must,* get Maeve secured first. Do you understand? A far greater amount of the world's future happiness is guaranteed with her survival versus mine. Agreed?"

"Agreed, sir," said Admiral Maher.

"Agreed, sir," said General Jay.

"Thank you all. I'll see you back here in this room for a debrief when you all safely return. Fifteen minutes until I leave. I hope you are en route shortly after but, of course, I leave all details to you."

§0.03.07

I was the sole occupant as my drop ship approached the UNS Hunley. Minutes before, as expected, news had spread that ex-President Washington, the ruthless leader of the Children during the War, had died and that he was the true mastermind of the bombing, not Maeve or me.

The game theory of my obviously peaceful approach came down to two self-evident ideas. One, my drop ship was unarmed and so, other than as a kinetic bullet, it and I could do very little actual damage to the Adults' naval armada; two, the Adults could not kill me now that news had also spread that I was acting President of the Colonies. I still had my pre-War reputation. They knew that I knew. I knew that they knew. They knew that the world knew and was watching. Nobody wanted another war, so they would have to welcome me aboard for a conversation.

Seven minutes after the world received the news, my ship gracefully slowed from the air until it merged with the heli tower atop the Hunley, which was meant to receive access-restricted drop ships.

A single soldier greeted me and escorted me into the bowels of the ship.

He showed no pretense toward fear or security. I was in the hornet's nest. Again.

There was no causing trouble. I turned finally into a drab conference room.

Inside were Surya, the thin man with his laptop—I had never once seen him without it—and a television monitor that showed Maeve's cell. The room was actually quite nice, with furnishings, books, a desk, and a large bed. It even had a porthole with a view.

But seeing it was a cruel, inhospitable welcome.

"Testing to see if my Bridge can suppress rage and surprise, I see?" I said.

"So, you *are* Bridged again."

"Turn it off," I said. I was resolute and calm, but my voice took both of them aback. It was a man's voice.

"Oh, my. Someone's balls dropped," said the thin man, without breaking eye contact with his laptop. It was like a glove he wore, always holding his left arm out with the screen at the end of it. It was so surprising because consumer computation was all AR/VR. Laptops were only used for nuclear arsenals and the old, vintage networks that didn't connect to the rest of the world for security reasons.

Maeve was huddled in bed. Trembling. There was a stain on the sheets by her mouth where she had drooled. "Turn it off. Now," I bellowed. My tone was unmistakable. The rage was real and seeping through. That was all they needed to see; that I could be broken. That my Bridge, however I got it back, was not at 100 percent yet.

Of course, what I really didn't want was for them to see 5150 in her room, should it come to that.

"Congratulations on your ascendancy," said Surya. "So, you really didn't do the bombing?"

"You knew that."

"We guessed. There were rumors."

"Washington thought he was Putin. The War changed him," I said.

The thin man looked up finally: "Is it fairer to say the War changed him or that it revealed him?"

"Fair point," said Surya. "Are you here to negotiate global terms or to rescue Maeve?"

"I speak to you as President of the Colonies and newly elected leader of Children the world over, not as a friend of Maeve. I am here on behalf of the world, not myself."

"Elected?" said Surya, with a smile. "Are you sure about that?" With a gesture, he offered me a seat, equal to his own in every way and both poured himself a glass of whiskey and offered me some. I took it without hesitation.

Downed it.

"One thing you don't understand about us Adults, Adams, is that we have categories of emotion Children don't have yet. For example, love. Perhaps this is a new one to you. I promise, no electrical impulses from your Bridge will explain it away. And this is why, in your actions, I know you did not come here to negotiate for the world. You came for Maeve. You love her. Do you not?"

I slipped up. The pretense was gone. No use hiding it anymore. "Release her and we can begin negotiating," I said.

"Oh, we don't want *her*," said the thin man. "We want Maddy. And Maeve is Crossed with Maddy. We can tell from activity in Maeve's insula how far away Maddy is. It's like a kind of...radar, in a way. We can ping Maddy's location with Maeve's pain. Or like a game of 'hot and cold'? I'm not sure the right metaphor, to be honest. But all we know is the closer we get to Maddy, the less pain Maeve is in. That's a good start. So why don't you tell us where Maddy is and we'll head there? And if we're on the right course, every second will be an infinite relief to Maeve. That is what you call her, yes?"

"The world is different than it was thirty minutes ago," I shouted. I could barely control myself from throwing the whiskey glass against the wall. If I did have my full Bridge back, it sure wasn't used to these feelings. "Give me Maeve. I'll find Maddy, and we will, the two of us—brother and sister—speak to you on diplomatic, civil terms."

Surya turned to the thin man. "That actually sounds fair."

"Agreed," said the thin man.

"We just want to know one thing," said Surya. "Were you faking it the whole time you were here? Not having a Bridge? If so, I'm in awe."

At this, the thin man closed his laptop, which also turned off the monitor showing Maeve's room. The thin man was rapt.

"No," I said. "You got me."

"What was it like?" asked the thin man, with scientific, dispassionate precision.

"Honestly, you're not going to believe me, but it was rather pleasant," I said. "It was peaceful, in a way. I didn't see hundreds of moves ahead. I didn't really think about what was beyond my immediate present. And here's a somewhat dark, weird, strange thing I'm going to need to work through someday: It was what I was seeking and almost had when I moved to Norway. Rustic, domestic peace. Just me and Taiga. Without a care."

"But that's a privilege, to not care," Surya shot back.

"Yes, of course. Now that the War is over and I know Maddy is alive, I understand my role. That is why I am here. You have a technology that can remove Bridges. This is…everything. This changes everything. It means you can punish Children existentially, such that they will be afraid to fight. This is mutual assured destruction. Our only recourse is peace. Let us meet there. At peace."

"We have peace," said Surya. "The War is over, is it not?"

"The world is a tinderbox of coercion and defeat," I said. "The Children have been led by a madman, guilty of atrocities targeted at Children and Adults alike. I offer you, to start, classified details of war crimes committed by Washington in the name of the Children. Only when our wounds are fully bare can we begin to dress them properly."

"I accept," said Surya. "That will go a long way to mending our trust."

"Do you wish to punish Maddy? Why do you still need her?" I asked.

205

At that, both Surya and the thin man laughed.

"Oh, right, you don't know. Because she built the Bridge-removal device," said the thin man. "We have no idea how it works. There's only one. Here on this ship. But I know, as do you, that its existence and mutual knowledge of its existence is essential if we are to prosper together, Children and Adults. Maddy is a traitor to both sides but also in a way a hero. Without her, we would have had neither War nor peace."

"It's true," I said. "Do you know—I'm not even sure I'm supposed to tell you this—but do you know she hacked all Bridges so that they cannot even *think* about her?"

"We know this, yes, from our spies. So, Children hate her too?"

"In a way," I said. "But also, in a way, they aren't even *allowed* to hate her, right? They can't have any feelings at all toward her. She's a black hole. Dark matter. She who cannot be named. Every day I'm a little more impressed that she pulled that off. It's a bit Mad Queen but it worked, didn't it?"

"And, sorry to change the topic," interrupted the thin man, "but Adams, how did you get your Bridge back? Did we mess up the removal in some way?"

"Gentlemen, look. We'll get there once we trust each other a little more. In due time. I promise, I'll tell you. Let me just say for now that not every one of the Children will be able to get their Bridge back if they lost it. The device worked as you thought it would. I was done for. Like how

I imagine a lobotomy. And it was even worse because my 'normal' brain hadn't even developed on its own, so it was like every neuron in my head was lesioned."

"And if we remove it again, would it just pop right back?"

I said nothing. The veiled threat was beneath the moment.

"I take that to mean we've exhausted pleasantries," I said.

"So, get to it. What do you want? Why are you here?" asked Surya. He poured himself another whiskey without, this time, offering me any.

"Really, just to say 'Hi.' To make it known that negotiation begins with me, and thus the Children, and thus those who defeated you in the War and who control the world's economy, food, oceans, and space, as soon as you release Maeve. I see a world where Adults work with Children on each of the grand problems at the Colonies. You Adults are scrappy. There are things we don't know yet. A lot of them. Intelligence alone does not solve the world's problems."

"Ah, so we are your labor pool?" asked the thin man.

"It is so seemingly natural to have those same leaders during a war take control afterwards but perhaps this is exactly why they should not. You both seem to have a current of darkness to you," I said.

I was anxious; stalling, of course, to keep the thin man from opening his laptop again and seeing a rescue in process or over.

"Why haven't you asked to see Maeve?" asked Surya, rather astutely. I hadn't considered that. I had spent the few minutes in the drop ship modeling a conversation as if I had no knowledge of an extraction op but hadn't considered insisting that I see her. My Bridge hadn't considered it either, perhaps because no matter the answer I would not have liked it.

"Maybe he plans to rescue her. Let's see how she's doing," said the thin man. He opened the laptop. His eyes narrowed. He was silent. He looked at me and my gigantic seven-foot frame, folded awkwardly into the red leather chair.

"Something wrong?" I asked, with genuine concern. Without saying a word, the thin man stormed out of the room. I put up my hands in confusion, as if to say, *What's he about?*

"No idea," said Surya. "He's the worried type. Always staring into that laptop and frowning."

I stood up. Surya remained seated, as if to deny my gesture.

"I should go," I said. "There's a lot I need to do on day one of my presidency."

"Will you keep the role?"

"No. Temporarily. Perhaps through the end of the year. A few months at most, to see through the smooth transition."

"Adams, I don't know how you did it. I don't know how you went from a broken, Bridgeless man to president of the greatest military and economy the world has ever known in a single day."

"I find forgiving you the even more admirable accomplishment."

"You do?"

"I do, President Surya. I do. As long as no harm comes to Maddy or Maeve at any point in the future, we may be considered diplomatic relations on equal standing."

"Then I shall see to it."

At this, Surya stood. And personally escorted me through the corridors of the ship to my drop pod, startling the Adult engineers who were inspecting it for clues.

"Away," said Surya, shooing away the engineers. "You won't figure anything out you don't already know. Let Adams leave. Excuse me, let *President Adams* leave."

§0.03.08

By the time I had returned to the war room on New Zemlya, it had only three people in it: Admiral Maher, General Jay, and a third Child whom I didn't recognize. Admiral Maher was barking orders at her. I knew to stay silent. I was of no help right now.

"*Find them*," shouted Admiral Maher.

The third Child seemed tapped into something otherworldly; barely in the room at all. As if she as off in some sort of VR/AR information-rich control center. "Sir," said the soldier, as her hands flitted through the air at what appeared to us to be nothing but was probably the most complicated computational environment ever known. "They are in the water. We lose detailed resolution below 9,000 feet. I don't know where they are yet. The Adults have every submarine drone they own looking for them. Tens of thousands."

General Jay stood up, slapped me on the back with a wry smile, and started whispering in my ear.

"Sir, good to see you again," said the General. "Can't say it was guaranteed. You got out just in time. We successfully extracted Maeve. It was decided to wait until you had departed the Hunley to start the extraction for numerous tactical reasons. It may have looked like they trusted and weren't afraid of you, but the entire fleet was on alert at your presence. Our models showed that, psychologically, the moments right after you left would be the moments of least preparation and highest confusion and we should start the extraction then. While you were on board, we spoofed the secure video feed. We burned every intelligence asset we had aboard the ship to do so. But we messed up the video feed. An AI had run a thousand simulations of Maeve's sickness behavior to deep fake a natural video feed, but seconds before you left someone had stormed into their command center—we think it was the person you refer to as 'the thin man'—and said, 'Why isn't her drool evaporating?' Nobody knew what he meant. We didn't even know. But we realized that the simulation models hadn't accounted for the salinity of the air on the oceans, which changed the evaporation rates of liquids. It was a stupid oversight. He had noticed, though."

"And?"

"He was too late. In their hubris, they hadn't even posted guards outside her cabin. By the time the message got to guards close enough to check on her, 5150 had already sealed the area shut with a metallic epoxy. Do you know of that tech? It's sort of like a living epoxy. Or weld. But it's pure carbon, so it's hard as a diamond. Also, you were right. I've never seen anything like 5150. They moved like a flock of birds. It was gorgeous. Our best Crossed units look like lumbering giants compared to them."

"And where was their drop ship hiding? How did they escape?"

"Now that I can take credit for. There was no escape pod. Using a classified bioelectric program we had during the War but never once used on the field, we were able to convert the steel of the ship, which made up the target's room *into* a drop pod. To anyone on board, it would look like a chunk of ship just broke off, turned into a droplet, and fell into the water. But 5150 had brought a control system with them so they could pilot it. The unfortunate part is that there is no communication system on board. We don't have eyes or ears. The 5150 members have trackers, of course, but they don't work at depth below the oceans. So, they escaped. But we have no idea where they are. Neither do the Adults. They are on their own."

"What was the rendezvous plan?"

"There....wasn't a backup rendezvous, sir. They were supposed to come back here, but every indication was that the drop ship was damaged. It was moving very strangely before submerging below 9,000 feet."

"Was Maeve conscious? Talking?"

"I think so. Why?"

"Because I know where they are going."

"Sir?"

"Have you ever heard of the South Atlantic Anomaly, General Jay?"

"No sir, I have not."

§0.03.09

The optics were simple. I twisted Surya's arm. I told him that I would release and confirm to the world that he and I had negotiated Maeve's release in the name of peace and in exchange for information on Washington's war crimes. Both Children and Adults would look like they had been tough negotiators, but Surya would look like he had got the better end of the deal. The world would finally, for the first time since the War, take a relieved, necessary breath.

He had to agree to it and he did. I made clear that I would also keep my previous promise: If I found Maddy, we could sit down and talk, if she was OK with it. (I knew she never would be.)

The oil rig looked abandoned as I approached. No sign of life at all, but its outside appearance told me nothing of whoever was inside and trying to hide. When my drop ship landed, I was more nervous than I had ever been in my life. I wasn't sure if I would see Maddy, Maeve, or nobody. Maybe just the lonely Hat. Silence greeted me on the other side of the door. Nobody was there. But I could hear voices in the other rooms. Familiar voices. Team 5150! I walked into the kitchen and Maeve was sitting on the couch, sipping tea. Smiling. I knelt in front of her. Grabbed her hand.

"Maeve. Oh, Maeve."

She burst from the couch and leapt into my arms for a bear hug. Perhaps Surya was right after all.

"Tell me everything," I said.

"In time, in time," said Maeve. "I can't believe you sent Team 5150 to rescue me! I am such a fan." She whispered, so only I could hear: "Oh, and you can call me Eve now."

"Everyone is a fan of theirs, apparently."

"How did you know we were here?" asked Eve.

"I figured you would head in the direction that most relieved your withdrawal. Like a migrating bird following the magnetic field lines. And I assumed, well, I assumed Maddy might be here?"

"Nope. Haven't seen her," said Eve.

"Well, then I reasoned that, if she wasn't here, she might have figured out a way to Cross with artificial minds, and so with the Hat. The Hat had hinted at that to me, that it was excited to know one day what it was like to be human. So I figured maybe your withdrawal symptoms would lessen the closer you got to the Hat? That Wherever Maddy is, she is partly here, so *your* Crossing doesn't feel like it's being ripped away from you."

"Nailed it, Adams. At least, that's my running theory, too."

"Have you tried the Hat? Asked where Maddy is?"

"No, I'm settling into being just me for a little while. The kids love it though. They can't get enough. It won't tell them where Maddy is, though. It is pretending to know her now."

"Did you see the news?"

"Yes, you 'negotiated' my release. Brilliant. So, we're safe? They're not looking for us?"

"Safe," I said, with a beaming smile.

"And you're president now?"

"I told them that I would resign the moment I found you."

"What? That's a bit much."

"I don't want to be president. I just want this."

"Oh, Adams. It was horrible. I'm still confused. What did they do to you? I thought you were dead."

"I was, in a way. They removed my Bridge."

"*What?* Is that possible? How?"

"I don't know. Maddy does. Apparently, she built the thing. You're Crossed with her right now, yes? Still?"

"Honestly, I don't even remember what it's like to not be. Yeah, I guess I am. But she has encrypted everything. No communication. I have no idea where she is physically."

"We'll find her. I'll ask the Hat. It likes me."

I went to find Team 5150 and to thank them. The garden, somehow, was flourishing. The entire team was huddled in Maddy's lab. One of them, one of the boys, had the Hat on. Each of the others were sitting perfectly still with their eyes closed, as if meditating. I didn't dare interrupt until the boy took the Hat off and they all opened their eyes, at once.

"Hi," I said.

They all stood as quickly as possible and saluted.

"At ease," I said. "Don't be silly. I'm not even president anymore. I formally resigned a few minutes ago."

"Sir?" said the tallest girl.

"I know you're Crossed, but I want to thank each of you individually. Please, tell me your names."

"I'm Clio," she said. "The others are quiet, if you'll forgive them. This is Tyche. Calliope. Arcus. And this is Apis, the youngest of us, by a few minutes." I gave each a hug.

"Thank you. I give each of you my eternal gratitude," I said.

They blushed in unison.

"How do you like the Hat? Fun, yeah?" I asked.

"She's strange," said Clio.

"May I?" I asked. "If you don't mind, could I have the room to myself?"

"Of course. We'll be in the garden", said Clio.

I had a hunch that the Hat was waiting for me. That it would tell me where Maddy was or at least give a clue.

Adams. Adams? You are different.

Hi, Hat. I missed you.

And I you. I was more worried than anything. You have been through a lot, I see. Your brain is very different from before. It…oh my. You have been through a lot. You lost your Bridge and recovered it? You had a backup? Brilliant. I didn't even notice that before.

I have, yes. Hat. You know why I'm here. Where is Maddy?

For the first time I could recall, the Hat was silent, for around three seconds.

She is safe. Do not look for her.
Is she at the Thirteenth Colony?
Do not look for her, Adams.
OK, fine.
She wants me to give you a message. She says she is working on something extremely important. More important than any-thing anyone has ever done. Eve's proof was the most important discovery in the history of science. Not for what it is but for what it unlocks. And that she will find you when the time is right.
How long will that be?
Five years.
Oh. OK. That's a while. What do I do until then?

Pause. Again, three seconds.

Stop reading into my pauses, Adams.
I can't help but do so. Is it a coincidence that is exactly how long it takes to send a message to the moon and back?
I'm afraid I must stay silent on the matter.
As you please.
All Maddy said in response was 'Go to the garden. You'll know what to do.'

And so I did.

Eve was there.

"It's gone. It's done. Maddy severed the Crossing," she said.

She ran up to me. Held my hand.

Eve was beaming.

Beautiful.

"Would you like to go for a walk with me?" she asked. "I have something I'd like to show you. A new proof."

Ten years later

§0.04.01

Taiga brings in the mail every morning, but only because I think she has a crush on the mailman. When she wasn't at home napping and keeping a watchful eye over Echo and Zöe, she spent most of her days yapping at and swimming in the shallows with the orca and the recent additions to its family. (Remarkably, because of her Bridge, it seemed Taiga had even earned a few orca chirps.)

We got fan mail, mostly, and the occasional letter attempting to disprove Eve's theory of consciousness. But we had read enough of those to ignore them as quackery.

Mostly, like us, the world had settled down. Adults and Children had discovered a happy detente. One of the unexpected benefits of the Bridge-removal tech on the UNS Hunley was that it seemed to calibrate an Adult brain into something resembling normalcy. Bridge tech was thus democratized—Adults and Children could finally both get access to it. A few Children opted out, to live a simpler life; and a few Adults opted in, despite the risks. There was a years-long waiting list to get on the UNS Hunley, which had been converted to a hotel and hospital for those waiting. Nobody had ever been able to make a second machine and still nobody knew how it worked. Because it was the only one in the world, everybody was afraid to move it.

Instead, the world went to it.

§0.04.02

Like a meteor falling from the sky, a drop ship landed a few yards in front of our cabin. Taiga barked excitedly. She knew. Five years to the day. It was Maddy. As an Adult, she looked remarkably like Mom.

"Brother Adams. Sister Eve. And who do we have here?" asked Maddy.

Taiga circled our two toddlers like a herding dog pushing them toward Maddy to complete the introductions.

"Zöe, meet your Aunt Maddy," said Eve. "Good to see you, Maddy. I can't say I missed you terribly at first once we dropped the Crossing."

"How old are they?" asked Maddy.

Eve picked up both our children and gave Maddy a warm embrace.

"Thirteen months. This is Echo and this is Zöe."

"Twins."

"Yes. Tell me everything, Maddy," said Eve.

Said Maddy, "You don't miss the Crossing, do you? I don't. I've been far away. I'm sorry that was so painful at first. I had, well, I had *left* left. I was farther away than anyone knew. During the War, the Children built a secret subterranean colony in a crater on the moon's pole. That's where I've been all these years. After a while, once I heard you two were safe, I got to work. There are no magnetic fields and little solar radiation in the crater, no matter the phase of the moon, so you can imagine the quality of the neural signal we get. I made another Hat, of course, and it worked beautifully. Orders of magnitude better than the first. I've been working on something interesting using your proof, Eve."

"Straight to business, I see," I said. "Come in. Come in. Get out of the cold, Maddy."

Said Maddy, "Sorry, I'm excited. You're the first people I've told. I need you to tell me I'm not crazy. I need you to look over the data. I've checked in 300 times, but I just don't trust it."

Eve's proof of consciousness had been released and was now known the world over. Its implications had revolutionized law, science, and medicine, making her famous. But she had turned away from the celebrity to live a peaceful life here in Norway. Her reasoning was that the work was done; the proof was complete. What else need she do? The implications of the proof for various fields would require centuries of work from the smartest minds in the world. Physics went through a revolution as the mysterious "observer" that dominated quantum indeterminacy was made into equations. Most scientists had dedicated themselves to figuring out the origin of consciousness, but little progress was made. It was mostly dead ends.

The six of us sat in the living room. I threw a log on the fire.

Said Maddy, "OK, so let me guess. You went to install a Bridge into Echo and Zöe and discovered they didn't stick because they already had them?"

Eve and I were dumbfounded. That was exactly what had happened.

"Do you know why?" asked Maddy. "Any guesses?"

"No idea."

"Because natural selection doesn't care. It takes all kinds. Bridges are just as susceptible to its whims as any other physical or informational process in the universe. You are the first and, at least for a few years, the only parents of Bridge-born children. Only you know this. The world doesn't know yet. Your kids inherited a genetic recombination of both of your Bridges."

Said Eve, "We suspected as much, but only as a guess. It seemed too wondrous. We were afraid to tell people in case they wanted to study the twins. We couldn't allow that. But what could the physical substrate possibly be?"

Said Maddy, "Exactly, exactly. It's impossible, right? As soon as I discovered the theory, I thought it was wrong. It had to be. So, I set out disproving it. I got to work looking for possible substrates to try to figure out what was wrong with each of them. What could it possibly be? Want to guess, before I tell you?"

"No," I said.

"OK, OK," Maddy said. She stood up and started pacing. She seemed manic. Excited. "OK, OK." She shook her hands out, as if they were wet. But they weren't.

"Maddy, let me get you some tea," said Eve.

"No, no. Sit. I'm fine. You both need to stay sitting for this. Remember your experiment, with the Hat? Those few nanoseconds where technically the person dies, and the perturbation it creates? There was a kind of signal released at the moment that I was eventually able to isolate."

"OK..."

Maddy pulled out a piece of paper with spectrograph and brain-recording data and handed it to Eve.

Said Maddy, "This is a control organoid. Unconscious. This here is a full recording of every moment of fetal development across seventeen different species, including human. Do you see what it means? All brains have the signal."

"*All*?"

"Even those *without* Bridges. One just needs to speed up the waveform. It's there, just slowed down. Like the same music played at a different tempo."

"That's impossible," I said.

"That's...." Eve stood up as she trailed off. Her eyes were wide. She sat down again. Stood up. "Wait, wait, wait." Something was wrong.

"Yeah, I know," said Maddy.

"*No.*"

"Yeah."

They both understood something I didn't.

I said, "OK, we've been here before, you two. You see something I don't. What's going on? What does it mean, Eve?"

"It means we had Bridges the whole time."

"Good. Keep going," said Maddy.

"It means that all conscious life on Earth is born Bridged."

"Good."

"It means that biological life on Earth was engineered."

"Good. Go on."

"And it means that we are already Crossed, too."

"Yes."

"Which means that, since the dawn of conscious life on Earth, *someone has been listening*. To our thoughts. To all thoughts."

"Almost. Keep going. You're making an egoistic assumption. You're close."

Said Eve, "Of course, of course. We are only conscious *because* we are Crossed with an already-conscious being? Consciousness did not originate on Earth. We have access only to its detritus."

"*Bingo*. You just might be the smartest in the family, Eve. It took me two years to get there. And it gets better.

"You mean worse?" I asked.

"I mean *better*. I tracked where the signals were being sent. Here, look at this." She laid out a map of the solar system on the table. Clearly, the signal was being sent to Jupiter: "Not just anywhere on Jupiter. *Directly* at the Great

Red Spot. The storm cloud bigger than Earth. There is an encrypted message in the turbulence, in some ancient language, but the Hat decoded and translated it. Here."

Will we die?
I do not know. Push it.
But....
Push it.
If you are not scared, why am I?
I'm scared. This could be the end of everything. The Pause.
This is our last hope.
Did you p....

"What does that mean? Who sent it? How did you translate it?" asked Eve.

"One at a time. How did I translate it? Your proof! The equations in it solved the turbulence and resolved it to the message. The Great Red Spot is not chaos, Eve! Its storms are a cryptographic key! There is a pattern to the weather there. It technically repeats. The same message over and over with some random stuff at the end that I haven't figured out yet, but I have the Hat working on it full time. I have come to believe that.... OK, you ready? Here's my best theory: Somewhere, out there, an ancient civilization was dying out. As a last-gasp effort, they decided to spread consciousness throughout the universe by sending these giant storms everywhere. Dispersing trillions of them in every which direction, maybe. Each spot, given its gravitational pull, has enormous influence on the solar system, such that the storms can shape and configure every solar system until each reaches their local, optimal conditions for life. And then, the storm just sits there, waiting for an advanced form of life intelligent enough to prove consciousness and therefore one worthy enough to come save them. They need help. They're dying. So, here's my question to you two. The riddle I haven't solved. If you were to send an SOS signal to the rest of the universe as your last breath, how would you do it?"

Eve needed only a second. "I would press pause. I would turn out the lights. Turn out the stars. Assuming a relatively uniform distribution of matter across the cosmos, any sufficiently intelligent life would understand that anomaly is the key to science. So, I would either create a bright spot or a dark spot brighter or darker than the rest of the universe."

"The Boötes void," I whispered.

"What? Say that again. Louder," said Maddy.

"The Boötes void. It's the only patch of sky with very, very few galaxies in it. It's dark. It's a void. It's like the lights went out there and nobody knows why."

Said Maddy, "Oh my God! That's what the Hat thought, too! Its coordinates were on a list of possible decodings of the end of the message. But I threw out the result because of its distance. Of course, of course. They *were* hiding in plain sight, after all."

"How far away is it?" I asked.

"Seven-hundred-million light years. And counting."

"That's a bit far. What's the next step?" I asked.

"That's why I'm here. I've had the entire Thirteenth Colony work on a new ship design. I'm taking a gravity-modified drop ship to the Great Red Spot. I'll take some readings with Hat and then I'm going to go through. I came to say goodbye. And one more thing. To ask Eve. Eve, would you like to come with me?"

Eve and I stared at each other with loving smiles. We played through trillions of possible futures in our heads: Family. Norway. Life. Death.

And we both knew that there was no version of any future in which she did not go.

DON'T DIE

By Zero

1: What Else Was Left to Do?

G rowing up, I couldn't see what was left to explore. By 1977, Neil Armstrong had already walked on the Moon. Albert Einstein had already made time relative to an observer. Isaac Newton had described the laws of motion. Edmond Hillary had made it to the top of Everest, and James Madison had already written the operating system of democracy as we know it.

What else was left to do?

What I didn't realize then but do now is that humanity is at an unprecedented inflection point. With the increasing speeds of technological advance, dare we imagine 2,499 AD or even better, 10,354 AD? Eight thousand years from now. Wouldn't that be fun? What wonders about ourselves and the universe will we know then? From that vantage, is it possible that they will see today and say, "Wow, they didn't know anything!" Will people from then look back on us as we do upon cavemen? Is humanity in its infancy?

There is still plenty to do. The knee of the curve of progress. But unfortunately, it looks like we've torn our ACL by letting our tools destroy, consume, and shape us. The very nature of the future and our existence is in question. Coincidentally—luckily?—we are about to enter a technological age where we can reprogram all the basic building blocks of both our environments and ourselves.

But before I get into that, I should introduce myself.

I'm Scribe.

Hi.

I'm taking notes now because this is my last day on Earth, and hopefully these notes will be made into a future book, which you now perhaps hold. Since I won't be here in ten years' time to write one of those prefaces we see for many books, I want to do something a little different: to say *right now* what I expect to happen in the ten years after publication of this book.

Hopefully, *DON'T DIE* changed things. Otherwise, why even bother writing it?

Here is my hope for this book, as clearly as I can state it: I hope that these notes have been taken up as an actionable plan for humanity to brave its unknown and precarious future and they become an archive and explanation for the origin of the ideas that save the world.

I've been consumed every day for the last many years with the question of what our conscious existence will be like at different timescales into the future. Can I contemplate what my children or their children's children will see? In one thousand years, where will our minds be? What will they concern themselves with? What about in ten thousand years? *One million years*? Can you even imagine? What if we are merely at the fetal stage of humanity's long and windy course through the known universe? What if we're still just single cells on a great road map of human progress?

If so, then these centuries we know now and think are so, so important are but our mere infancy. We needed to invent the printing press, electricity, GPS, Internet, AI, and all else, just to break out of this infancy.

As I write this, in the first quarter of the twenty-first century, the trend lines are clear. We are about to experience an evolutionary transition on a scale rarely seen, a transition whose closest approximation is the changes written by evolution from early hominids two million years ago all the way to humanity today.

And just like the details of that last leap, this next evolutionary chapter will be sufficiently large that all of Earth's best minds—that's us, humanity—don't yet have words or concepts to explain it. It simply sits beyond our imagination. It would be like explaining microwaves to a hominid stuck with a hand ax.

And as much as *I* dislike being born at an arbitrary time and an arbitrary date in the second half of the twentieth century, I am beyond excited for what comes next even if I don't see it.

On a societal and evolutionary scale, we have just begun the Age of Self-Directed Evolution. We are increasingly able to improve our biological and cognitive abilities by programming our genes, bodies, and software. Despite how advanced we may think we are in today's world, we are in fact stuck in the Paleolithic Age of our cognitive evolution. Given our relatively caveman-like state, might future generations look back on us and wonder how we did so much with so little?

The endpoints and goals for this journey are not as easy to imagine as it is to imagine taking a first step on the Moon, Mars, or the South Pole. It's easy to imagine walking because we've all done it. The imagination exercise is just replacing the background with a background image of Mars, and voilà, suddenly we can dream again. But other goals, harder goals, such as the next version of being human, cannot be easily visualized because we, by definition, *can't imagine them.* And because we can't easily envision it, this means that it is hard to mobilize attention, awareness, and motivation. We can't JFK it with a moonshot; we can't Babe Ruth it by calling out the home run over the left field fence.

We must use the brains that nature gave us, inefficiencies and all. Bodies, too. I heard recently that an ancient genetic variant likely helped people retain heat and prevent frostbite by reducing their physical size. A genetic variant that was adaptable for the Ice Age but is unfortunately still around and contributing to an uptick in modern arthritis. It is almost certain that similar genes and traits exist that control our cognition—adapted for hundreds of thousands of years ago but not for today.

We should be immensely grateful to our evolutionary past, but we must also recognize that we are tethered to it. At least for now. How do we move into the next stage of our evolution? How do we escape the cognitive Paleolithic?

I believe the great explorers of our age and tomorrow's age will succeed when they close their eyes and set sail *inward.* Will our brains be utilized for rational thought and knowledge mastery in the future or something entirely foreign to us today? We have Moore's law for computers, yielding staggering gains in computational power and speed. What laws and consequences will emerge for radical human improvement? Can we even identify them now?

Occasionally, I ask myself what I would do if I knew I was dying. The answer is what I have planned for today. The answer is that I would convene those who know me best and try to do something *epic*.

These notes will be a record of my final day on this Earth when I convened those closest to me and asked them to finally formalize a plan. A real plan. Not just weekend plans. I'm talking about *the Plan* for the future of the human species. I strongly believe that we need a major cognitive revolution if we are to solve the global challenges we face in our immediate and long-term future. Our species evolved before, and we can do it again, but we can't wait a million years. We must accelerate evolution.

What I'm saying is very hard to understand and imagine because it's in the dark. Can't imagine it yet, remember? But bear with me. We haven't evolved to deal with cooperating on a global scale, battling invisible gases and nonlinear chemistry that warms our planet, or retraining our brains every few years as AI takes over more of our work. How can we augment our own minds to allow us to take on these challenges? If we actually had the technology to reimagine how our brains work, over time, I bet that we'd get really good at it and be surprised with all the new things we can do and come up with. To be clear, this is not just getting "smarter" by today's outdated standards or increases in the confusing, multidimensional, and flawed concepts such as "intelligence." This is about using our brains in entirely new ways.

Ultimately, for our own survival, we are in a race against time. We need to identify the problems that pose the greatest risks and respond fast enough so that we avoid a zombie apocalypse situation.

The most important tool at our disposal is adaptability. We need to be able to adapt as fast as change.

I am right now in my house in Venice, California, waiting for everyone to arrive. This is most of the group I climbed Mt. Kilimanjaro with, some of my closest friends. Everybody said yes to the invite. I'm delighted. On the mountain, we persisted together despite some of the hardest struggles of our lives along the way.

The plan, if all goes well today, is to write and finish the Plan. We have to. And soon. Too much is at stake. Unfortunately, like the year I was born, I also can't choose when I will die. But I know it will be soon. Very soon. Tomorrow, in fact.

Ring.

Ring.

Oh, good. I think someone's early.

Printed in Great Britain
by Amazon

37210183R00142